Edwin Edgerton Aiken

The Secret Society System

Edwin Edgerton Aiken

The Secret Society System

ISBN/EAN: 9783337770150

Printed in Europe, USA, Canada, Australia, Japan

Cover: Foto ©Andreas Hilbeck / pixelio.de

More available books at **www.hansebooks.com**

THE

SECRET SOCIETY SYSTEM

By E. E. AIKEN.

NEW HAVEN:
PUBLISHED BY O. H. BRIGGS.
1882

PREFACE.

A large part of this work first appeared as a series of five articles in the *Yale Critic* of 1882. The question discussed has been thought of sufficient importance to warrant republication in more permanent form, and accordingly the articles have been revised and enlarged for this book. While the principles given are believed to be true for all communities, they have been discussed with especial reference to secret societies in colleges.

NEW HAVEN, June, 1882.

TO

F. A. BECKWITH,

YALE, '78.

CONTENTS.

INTRODUCTION.

When one has enjoyed the advantages of the college course, it is no gracious task to make any public criticism involving the institution to which he owes so much, and which he has honored and loved; but there are principles of fidelity which transcend all personal considerations, and the statement of the truth is sometimes the highest service. Great and noble as our foster-mother is, it is in behalf of a larger and a nobler life within her walls, and in all other communities as well, that these words are written.

Still less gracious is it to utter criticism upon institutions whose honors and privileges one has shared, and whose trusts have been confided to his keeping; and perhaps, in view of the peculiar nature of the institutions in question, it will be simple justice for me to say, at the outset, that the organization, with whose membership I was honored in Senior year, was almost ideally perfect, of its kind. I do not see how any organization of that sort could have been much better.

But institutions exist for men, not men for institutions; and though loyalty to an institution is an important principle, yet loyalty to the truth is one far more sacred. Every man—particularly every young man—must be granted the right to change his party with his convictions. The opposite principle stifles all freedom and honesty, and it may be added that secret societies have a tendency to this which is not in their favor. The first principle was recognized in the many changes of party at the time of our late

war. There were new circumstances, but new
facts and principles should be as potent as new
circumstances; perhaps more so. Luther doubt-
ingly[1] entered a monastery, and lived a monk for
some years; but he was not thereby kept from
speaking the truths of the Reformation. In
English history, Charles James Fox was driven
by his convictions "to detach himself from his
early surroundings;" and "he dissolved his
partnership with Sandwich and Wedderburn,
and united himself to Burke and Chatham."[2]
So acted Mr. Gladstone, and English Protestants
were surprised "when one who took so high a
view of the duties and privileges of the Established Church, became, a generation later, an
advocate for the disestablishment of the Irish
branch of that church."[3] In 1845, to form an
impartial opinion, said Mr. Gladstone,[4] "I have
separated myself from men with whom, and
under whom, I have long acted in public life,
and of whom I am bound to say * * that I
continue to regard them with unaltered sentiments both of public regard and private attachment."

It is involved in this principle that the right
of free discussion and action is in no way for-
feited. It is limited by the obligation not to use
against a party what has been confided to one
as a member of it, and that obligation I shall
always recognize.

A discussion of this topic violates what has
come to be one of the first rules of college eti-

[1] Life, p. 9.
[2] Trevelyan's Early History of Fox, p. 452.
[3] Smith's Life of William Ewart Gladstone, p. 73.
[4] Do., do., pp. 85, 86.

quette; but for this—not a light matter—there is ample warrant. Whether political or not, these institutions in college are practically public, not private; their influence, whether so intended by them or not, is a great, in some instances perhaps the great factor in college life; and every year they look for support from the incoming or lower classes. I hold that bodies of men have no right to establish institutions whose influence is as public and far-reaching as that of those in question, and demand that nothing shall be publicly said about them. The right of free discussion of public matters is one of the guarantees of our liberty, for which our fathers fought; "one of the most precious and necessary rights of the individual, and one of the indispensable elements of all advancing humanity; * * * an element of all civil liberty," says Francis Lieber,[1] the able and patriotic author of the work on civil liberty used as a text-book by the Yale seniors; and in the name of freedom I claim and exercise this full right.

The need of some discussion of this subject rests on this principle: that men should understand the principles and tendencies of the institutions which they are called on to support. Now under the class system, particularly, college classes are held for years, without being in a position to understand its nature, which may even make some discussion of this a public duty. Graduates and college officers, also, often give the system active or virtual support, when it is probable that they would not, if they under-

[1] Civil Liberty, p. 87; see also Chapter XIII, on Publicity.

stood its real character and influence. Moreover, open debate is most healthful in its influences; it opens the windows of the mind and
lets the truth come streaming in like the sunlight.

It is unfortunate that none who are identified
with the system will enter the debate, though
Baird does close his book on *"American College
Fraternities,"* with a defense cf them. But if
none of their members will appear, this cannot
be laid to the charge of any one else; and here,
too, it may be added that this principle of refusing to appear before the tribunal of public opinion, is not in favor of the secret societies. The
nature of them may afford some explanation of
their silence; but this mode of proceeding is
not in harmony with the spirit of republican
institutions, and the societies should have good
reason for doing that which, before the law,
would certainly bring judgment against them
by default, if for no other reason.

CHAPTER I.

—Sweet bells jangled, out of tune and harsh.—*Shakspeare*.

The great normal organizations of human society are three: the family, the state, and the church. The school is another great institution, which may be placed here as coming next in importance. I propose to consider this subject somewhat in relation to each of these, and first, in its family and social relations.

The college years lie between the breaking of old family and social ties and the forming of new ones. During this period, the existence of college societies "in some form is a necessary outgrowth of human nature."[1] Both intellectual and social instincts reach out for that satisfaction and development which is attained in association with one's fellows. Says Ex-Gov. Hawley, of Connecticut, "the fitness and capacity for friendship, and the ability to attract and retain true friends, are as well subject to cultivation and improvement, as any quality or power of mind."[2] Come now the secret societies, and offer to meet these wants; "and in this culture" in friendship, continues Ex-Governor Hawley, "lies one of the chief values of the college fraternities." And according to Baird,[3] the "constitutions of the widest

[1] Porter's American Colleges, p. 194.
[2] Psi Upsilon Catalogue, p. x.
[3] American College Fraternities. pp. 197–198.

and best known societies " would proclaim essentially the two objects of satisfying the intellectual
and social nature.   Let us consider the methods
employed; we notice that a leading characteristic is secrecy ; why are the societies secret?

1. The societies may possess truths of value,
political, religious, scientific, social, or of some
other kind.   " There are mysteries within the
INNER veil of our altars," writes a member of
one organization,[1] " that none except the members of the fraternity are permitted to behold.
Solemn and sublime truths are there inculcated,
that have never reached the ear of any save those
who have proved themselves worthy of the sacred
trust."   But when the origin of most of these
societies is considered, their possession of such
truths seems rather improbable ; and in view of
their limited membership, the claim of including
either all or any large part of those able to appreciate them, seems equally unfounded.   It is
hard to see why such truths would not be as valuable to the world at large as to the societies;
and if they would, the spirit which withholds
them is wrong, and contradicts the very nature
of truth, which is for all, like the sunlight.
Says Lieber, " In the early stages of society it
can be easily imagined that the ignorance and
vehement superstition of the whole people at
large should make it necessary to make of some
great religious truth, for instance the belief in
one God, perhaps introduced from some distant
and more advanced region, a mystery, for fear
that if not kept as such it would soon be entirely

[1] American Pamphlets, Yale Library, Vol. 3, Constitution
of Lodge, I. O. O. F., p. 7.

eradicated. So likewise may certain scientific truths, militating with the common belief, be exposed to total extirpation by fanaticism, if not kept within a circle of initiated persons; but it seems that knowledge and religion with the white race have become so diffused that no such mysteries are any longer necessary, and that we are thus likewise spared the dangers to which these societies must always expose themselves as well as others." [1]

2. Secrecy may be used to create and strengthen friendship. The binding force of a common secret is a well-known fact; it rouses the instincts of fidelity and honor, and marks off its possessors as a circle by themselves, more or less distinctly according to its nature. Nevertheless, though usually incidental to friendship, it is not its true foundation; which is virtue, first. as Cicero repeatedly insists in his Essay on Friendship, and, second, adaptability of character and purpose. The sharing of a secret makes a bond, but it is a very different one from that of a generous friendship. It is like the external force which holds two soldiers together in the ranks, while they may be hating each other in their hearts. Neither does an artificial secrecy, as distinguished from the keeping of spontaneous confidence, materially strengthen friendship If the inward and spiritual bond exists, it will unite; if it does not, the external and mechanical contrivance of secrecy can never take its place.

3. The secrecy may be employed to exert the power of mystery over the outside world, the

[1] Political Ethics, 2d edition, Vol. II, p. 196.

societies thus becoming "invested with a facti- tious importance."[1] There is a wonderful power in mystery which makes the human mind sub- ject to its spell. Let it be known that Dick and Harry have a secret, and immediately all the other boys are agog to find out what it is. If it be very mysterious, it even holds their minds in a sort of awe under its power, until they can solve the mystery, when they are content. But this operation does not often reflect any credit on the two boys; and if this is the purpose of the college secrecy, it is certainly an unworthy device to gain the dignity for an association which should be won by its own character and purpose; for the importance here would depend entirely on the concealment, and not at all on the thing concealed. This might be commen- surate in dignity to the impression made, but it might also fall very much below it; and Presi- dent Porter therefore calls this importance "fac- titious."

4. Secrecy may be intended to conceal doings which will not bear the light. To this Baird[2] replies that the concealment in college frater- nities is not sufficient. Certainly their secrecy is far from complete, but there is more than enough to meet the above purpose. His second reply is, "Given a number of college students, whose tastes, habits, antecedents and prospects are known, to determine what would be their actions when assembled together for their own purposes. The dullest college officer, the oldest trustee, could solve it immediately. We thus see this

[1] Porter's American Colleges, p. 195.
[2] American College Fraternities, pp. 196–197.

great bar of secrecy removed and vanishing."
But, unfortunately, we do not. For some institutions this answer is satisfactory. It could not
be supposed for a moment that the men who
compose them would be united for such an object ; but this does not hold in many cases, and
there is always the question as to which element
of an organization controls. There can be no
doubt that this is the use made of some secret
organizations, and the opportunities afforded by
secrecy are such as to make this in some instances its probable object.

5. The secrecy may simply aim to secure the
privacy required for social purposes. "To the
question why any secrecy?" Ex-Gov. Hawley
replies,[1] "why do even two friends habitually
seek occasions to converse with each other
only?" It is true that privacy is usually a condition of society, and sharing of confidence, of
friendship; but the condition is not the foundation, in either case. Whereas the secret society
theory carries the principle too far, and so perverts it, first by carrying the privacy and confidence over into an artificial secrecy, which is
distinct from either of them, and second, by
making this, apparently, the foundation of society and friendship. It is further urged that
families and all other organizations hold secret
conferences. In reply, if the societies resorted
to secrecy as families and most organizations
do, no objection could be made; but they do
not. The family resorts to secrecy as an occasional expedient, dictated by circumstances; it
has secrets, but it is not essentially a secret soci-

[1] Psi Upsilon Catalogue, p. xi.

ety. Should it become such, the social life of the community would be spoiled. The secret society takes a true principle and perverts it. Instead of holding an occasional secret conference, as circumstances require, it makes secrecy a ruling principle. Its secrecy is not occasional and temporary and natural, but artificial and permanent; which makes a wide difference. While the great proportion o experiences in family and friendship may be freely talked of, no mention of society experiences must be made. Further, the privacy is an ostentatious privacy; as if two friends should publish a notice that they were about to exchange confidences, and warn everybody off; thus violating the very spirit of privacy. The mistake rebuked by our Lord, in the case of those who sought divine communion on the corners of the streets, is paralleled in this method of seeking earthly communion.

Now some of these objects are perfectly natural and right: but to artificial secrecy as a means of obtaining them, there are grave objections, on social grounds alone. Secrecy is not calculated to preserve that student character, "frank and transparent, open and fearless," around which friendships gather, and which President Porter apparently commends.[1] There is a certain charm and romance about mystery, but it has also a strangeness and repression which chill and deaden social feeling. "Secrecy and concealment ever afford grounds for suspicion," a feeling most fatal to friendship. Our honored Ex-President Woolsey declares the

[1] American Colleges, p. 175.

secret system "averse to the English character."
In view of such considerations, the social value
of an artificial secrecy is certainly open to very
serious question.

A second characteristic of this social system
is its exclusiveness. On this point Ex-Governor
Hawley says, "all men around us" have not " a
right to complain that each does not freely bare
his heart to all others." [1]   "It is not expected
that " "cordial, mutual pledges " " shall be made
to all ; it is right to choose those to whom they
shall be made." It is true that every social relation must have its limits ; but, speaking generally, there are great natural principles which
will mark them off without the use of exclusiveness. "Birds of a feather flock together," runs
the proverb, and under the operation of this
principle society will naturally adjust itself.
Exclusiveness is a perversion of these principles. As selfishness in the individual life perverts the true principle of selfness, or proper
regard for one's self, so exclusiveness makes
precisely the same error in the social life, by
making a selfish use of the social capacities.
It is harder to detect, perhaps, because it is on
the higher plane of social relations. But
error is possible in every sphere of action,
and because social relations are on a higher
level than personal relations, error in them is
none the less real. In general society, exclusiveness is considered a wrong characteristic
either of a person or a set, and it should not be
regarded more favorably when it is the characteristic of an organization. In this kind of or-

---

[1] Psi Upsilon Catalogue, p. xi.

2

ganization it does not spring altogether from smallness of numbers, which would characterize almost any circle of friends; but from want of flexibility and naturalness in the method of choice, and from the secrecy which isolates its members. Hospitality, that great principle which throws the warmth and kindness of the family life around its guests, and diffuses those beneficent influences which make the atmosphere of a home, is offered by the societies most scantily, or not at all; in fact, is essentially contrary to their principles. The secret society is exclusive because it is inhospitable and uncommunicative, while its methods of choice almost always break the natural lines of affinity and friendship.

A third question may now be raised, perhaps reaching more deeply into the social relations of this subject than either of the others. Is a formal association of any kind, for social purposes, based on true principles? A social object seems legitimate, and a formal association a proper method of attaining it; nevertheless, in most cases, I conceive this method to be an unnecessary and mistaken one. Ex-Governor Hawley says,[1] "There is a great positive value in the cordial, mutual pledges of confidence, assistance, trust, encouragement, equality, fidelity and honor." But as to social value, formal pledges are hollow, and cannot promote friendship, except as they express natural relations; as in that famous friendship which has charmed the world, "Jonathan and David made a covenant, because he loved him as his own soul."[2]

[1] Psi Upsilon Catalogue, p. xi.
[2] I Samuel, xviii: 3.

The covenant, however, sprang out of the friendship, not the friendship out of the covenant.
The difference in the positions of the two friends,
also, was a special reason for a covenant in their
case.   This can rarely be made on such a foundation of fitness for lasting friendship, and when
the sorrowful discovery is made, as it frequently
is, that such fitness does not exist, such a covenant forms a most awkward bond.   The general
truth is that the spiritual bond is the true one,
and that covenants of friendship are unnecessary; the compacts are to be made for different
ends.   In a social club, it is very hard, in the
first place, to make the formal lines correspond
to the natural relations, a difficulty much in-
creased when the club is formed not by those
whom it is to unite, but by others; and, secondly,
an element of selfishness easily creeps in which
tends to demoralize the organization.   I believe
that in many college organizations now defunct,
the first step to destruction was taken when the
social element took the reins to the dethrone-
ment of the intellectual.   "I hate the prostitu-
tion of the name of friendship to signify modish
and worldly alliances," writes Emerson.[1]   "Society is spoiled, if pains are taken, if the associates are brought a mile to meet."   As living
for happiness certainly defeats its own object,
and the rule is to live for God, when happiness
will come incidentally, so in most cases friendship thrives best without a formal organization,
as an incident to associations for other purposes.
These considerations have special force in a college, whose very aim is to develop the highest

[1] Essays, 1st Series, p. 188, 122.

and truest character and relationship.   It should
be noted, however, that the argument against
the present system does not depend on this last
point.   Even if the value of purely social organizations were admitted, many of the objections
to this form of association would still hold.

The three points already named properly de-
fine a secret society as a secret and exclusive
league.   This may exist for several objects ; but
I have considered it first in its social aspect, because in this country, and particularly in the
colleges, I believe this to be on the whole the
prominent feature of the system, though it has
also political and intellectual relations of importance.   These organizations are essentially
the same in college and out of it.   There is
much confusion of mind on this point; and
many regard college societies as different from
those without.   So they are, in some respects.
They do, to some extent, make homes instead
of breaking them up, and they are much more
intellectual.   Nevertheless, these are only modifications, not essential differences.   In the great
essentials above named the two are the same,
and they have also many other characteristics
in common.

The working of this, as a social system, in
college, may now be considered.   Only those
who have lived under the class system can understand its power over the lower classes.   With
the sight of the pins, at the beginning of the
course, curiosity is awakened, and already men
begin to feel those influences which cast their
mysterious shadow over the college life.   " Still
waters run deep," and though an observer might
not suspect it, many men are entirely subject to

this mysterious power. They must form natural friendships, but they look for a day of separation, and the shrewder ones are seeking to arrange for that. Thinking that popularity has a high value, they are led to use their friends as stepping-stones. The tendency is to use the sacred relation of friendship in a struggle for position. If a man has good prospects, men count him their friend ; if not, they neglect him ; and the hollowness of such friendship with the bitterness of such neglect need not be described. " Selfishness, an eye to business, vanity, frivolity, gluttony, and a love of mystery-mongering, concealed under the specious pretense of brotherly love, and longing for instruction—these are the motives that lead men into the lodge." [1]   Give ambition a leading place, and omit one or two of the others, and these are the motives which this system makes powerful in under-class life. When such motives control, as they often do, selfishness becomes supreme and friendship insincere. "Could the continuity of many of these societies," says President Porter,[2] "from one college year to another, be broken up, the college life would be greatly ennobled." The principle of "every man for himself," always too strong, is much intensified. A cordial, friendly spirit is killed, and many men graduate with an under-consciousness that they have never felt at home in college, and that a great part of the happiness of their college days has been somehow lost ; natural results of a social system which I believe inherently selfish. A

[1] Heckethorn's Secret Societies, Vol. I, p. 389.
[2] American Colleges, p. 195.

Yale paper once said editorially, [1] the societies "furnish the chief incentive to that trickery which seams under-class life through and through, dividing it into castes, and engendering in it bitter and undying alienations." Any competition might develop something of this, but the insincerity and personal bitterness are largely due to the societies.

Under the class system, fraternal feeling between the classes is very much diminished. Class distinctions would always limit this, but many a friendship which would give pleasure and profit to both parties, is either prevented or put on such awkward terms as to make it really worthless. The under-class man, however disinterested may be his regard for his society friend, feels as if he were somehow galvanized whenever he comes near him. Between the temptation to seek favor, and his resolve to maintain his own self-respect, his real friendship has a hard time of it, and can get little or no development. If a society man takes an honor, his under-class friend feels that his position will not allow him to congratulate him. Moreover, if he thinks himself a candidate, and it is a singular fact that most men privately do, he imagines himself the constant object of a critical inspection, which is quite enough to complete the galvanizing process above referred to. This is very unnatural, and there is here a general loss for which it is very doubtful if any gain within the narrow society lines can atone.

It would seem that the men in the societies could hardly fail to derive great benefits, both

[1] *Yale Courant*, March 23, 1878.

in development of social qualities and of friendships, and in acquaintance with graduates.
" One of the most valuable adjuncts of a college
life," says Ex-Governor Hawley, of his " dearly
beloved Psi Upsilon brotherhood." [1]   But—and
this point must be emphasized, for it is not understood—graduates mistake in thanking the
secret society for many friendships which they
do not owe to that, essentially, but to natural
relations in the college life.   The society is
largely the occasion, not the cause ; some other
occasion would do nearly or quite as well.
Drawbacks must also be found in the diversities
of character often united.   " Men have confessed
to me," said a graduate of a Southern college,
" that they had as much love for the devil as for
some of their fraternity associates."   The feeling
of what would be required by honor and loyalty
to the fraternity would keep most men from be-
traying any such sentiment ; but it seems certain
that it must often exist.   A college president
writes, the societies " put men socially, in regard
to each other, into an artificial and false position.
Their tendency is to lead men to associate only
with a small number with whom they may have
been thrown by accident, and to narrow the
intellect and the feeling." [2]   There is also a loss
in the isolation from the uninitiated.   Tennyson's verse,—

> —" he that shuts Love out, in turn shall be
> Shut out from Love."

is fulfilled, both in the individuals who support

[1] Psi Upsilon Catalogue, p. x.
[2] Hitchcock's Reminiscences of Amherst, p. 323.

this system, as society men, and in their organizations. There is, indeed, mutual forbearance,
whereby many friendships with neutrals continue; but never without some loss, while many
are weakened and some broken. Some of this
would exist under any system; but the societies
are responsible for much jealousy and hatred in
what should be an open, generous rivalry.
Many men are not specially affected, but the
general influence is to create a spirit of bitterness. "They have led to greater unkindness
and ill-feeling than almost anything else in college," says a college president. [1] It may be
remarked here, that one feature helping to create the bitterness which prevails, is the wearing
of badges; which is generally a violation both
of good taste and good manners. Of good taste,
because manhood needs no badge of its nobility,
nor friends of their friendship; of good manners, because it is a constant reminder to others
of distinction which they have failed to win.
Said a Yale paper, though in a year of high feeling, "the popular attitude toward the senior
societies is either bitterness or idolatry ; *   *
bitterness if you did not go, idolatry if you
did." [2] With class societies, this is modified by
old friendships, and much suppressed by pride
and the consciousness of nearly every man, that
he would have gone if he could. But a great
deal of it exists. "The whole university of
Cambridge," declares a Yale graduate, who spent
five years there, "does not contain as much
hatred, envy, malice and uncharitableness, and
general ill-feeling, as an American college." [3]

[1] Hitchcock's Reminiscences of Amherst, p. 324.
[2] *Courant*, March 23, 1878.
[3] Bristed's Five Years in an English University, p. 415.

The class system is also responsible for the heart-breaking disappointments which sadden the college on election days, and for the general depression resulting from an exclusion so utter and so hopeless; while friends and classmates are gone in, each man feels himself left out in the cold, and forever. I do not regard this argument as conclusive, because disappointment is incidental to a large part of life; but an artificial system must be judged by all of its effects, and this one is both deep at the time and far-reaching in its consequences.

To the alumni there is both gain and loss, for another element in these organizations is their perpetuity. The distinctions made in college are life-long, and the element of secrecy must always keep them considerably marked. Such a fraternizing as that of Linonians and Brothers, at the former's Centennial in 1853, is inconceivable under the secret system. Outside the college town some benefit may derived from the chaptered fraternities, and doubtless, as the years go by, the societies diminish and the college increases in importance with the graduates; but it seems evident that harmful barriers must long exist. Graduates living in their college town, or returning to it, must find their societies pleasant. There is a legitimate demand for something of this kind; but limited and exclusive societies are certainly very inadequate for meeting it, to say nothing of the positive harm done by reviving the old unpleasant feelings in the minds of neutral classmates. Many, perhaps, revisit their college who would not do so if it were not for the societies; but it is said that on the whole they have in this college di-

minished the attendance at Commencement. I
can only speak generally here, but it seems very
natural that the memories of exclusion, and the
knowledge that it would still exist, should influence many, perhaps unconsciously, to stay away,
and indications have led me to believe that such
is frequently the case. "One alumnus of Yale
cannot come back to his college with the same
freedom and pleasure as" another, says a recent
graduate, in reference to this system. Whether
the loss overbalances the gain, in this particular,
I do not undertake to say.

Taking a general view of this as a social system, it has some advantages, but also grave de-
fects; and many of these are not incidental, but
spring from its very nature. In general, even
if the advantages to the members are incalculable, as it is said in some instances they are, a
system which works good only to its members,
and evil to the non-members, cannot be based
on right principles. Such a system must con-
tradict the principles of reciprocity and mutual
helpfulness, on which life is founded. A literary
or athletic association usually comes into relations of mutual advantages with the public; and,
moreover, diffuses certain beneficial impulses.
But a secret society diffuses nothing whatever;
its very essential principle is to diffuse nothing.
Again, if the friendship within were the greatest
conceivable, the gain due to the society would
be far less than the general loss. If one great
object of this system is to promote fraternal
feeling, as Baird says it is, taking its effect as a
whole it signally fails.

CHAPTER II.

A ruddy drop of manly blood
The surging sea outweighs,
The world uncertain comes and goes,
The lover rooted stays.
—*Emerson.*

Few things are more delightful in experience, or more dear to memory, than the friendships of college days. Growing up between hearts young and noble, full of hope and enthusiasm, they fill college life with happiness, and their memory stays in the heart like some rare perfume, fragrant till the last hours of life.

The foundation of friendship is virtue. " It is Virtue alone that can give birth, strength and permanency to friendship," writes Cicero in his charming essay.[1] There is an attraction in virtue, that by a secret and irresistible bias, draws the general affections of those persons toward each other, in whom it appears to·reside." Any friendship worth the name must be based on mutual respect. The second requisite is adaptability of character and purpose. Out of this spring the confidences which are so delightful and healthful to the whole nature, and which are confidences because there are very few within the reach of any one man who have followed out the deeper lines of experience which are parallel to his own, and so can understand and sympathize with him. True friendship, therefore,

---

[1] Essay on Friendship, pp. 305, 266.

needs no exclusiveness; rarely can any one enter its charmed circle, and he who can belongs there. "We talk of choosing our friends, but friends are self-elected." Nor do they need much contrivance for coming at one another. "Friends also follow the laws of divine necessity; they gravitate to each other, and cannot otherwise."[1] "Genuine friendship, being produced by the simple efficiency of nature's steady and immutable laws, resembles the source from whence it springs, and is forever permanent and unchangeable."[2] A third element usually enters into friendship—that of time; friends must be summered and wintered, known in adversity and prosperity, in many relations of life, before their affection is strong and permanent. Hence, organizations to promote friendship are a resort to unnatural and forcing processes, like those of the hot-house; whereas, true friendship is a hardy plant, and thrives best on the rugged soil of effort.

Now the very organization of school and college is most favorable to the growth of friendship. To begin with, the college itself is a great family. Its members are all chosen men at the start, and more and more as the years go by; and presumably gentlemen. They are at an age when lasting attachments are easily formed. Says Whewell, [3] "at that crisis of life, when the vigor of manly thought blends with the warmth of youthful susceptibility," the student "acquires a number of subjects of common interest, of agreeable retrospect, of endearing recollection;

[1] Emerson's Essays, 2d series, p. 122.
[2] Cicero's Essay on Friendship, p. 250.
[3] University Education, p. 88.

and these points of union bind together the university men of the same standing by a tie which rarely loses its hold, or its charm, during their lives." The class organization of the American college is a strong bond between all its members. It takes the place of the college bond that unites the students in the various colleges which make up the English universities. Living in dormitories brings men into close and constant social relations. Multitudes of organizations unite still more closely—eating clubs, boating, ball and other athletic associations, the papers, musical clubs, religious, literary and art societies—all uniting men in ways most favorable to friendship. Besides the more permanent clubs, temporary organizations of a more or less private nature easily spring up between those of like tastes, which attain the same ends. "The true type of a Cambridge club," writes a Harvard graduate who studied at Cambridge, "is one where a certain body of students, interested in one object, unite to carry out that object, and are ready to admit anybody who cares for it too, and want nobody who does not. And the perfect example of these is in the clubs for athletic sports."[1] This I believe the true system, under which social relations will be natural and spontaneous, and a source of the highest benefit and happiness to the community.

To these natural relations, under the principles above given, students owe their friendships, and only to a very limited extent to artificial social systems. The life-long friendship between Ex-President Woolsey and Dr. Leonard Bacon

[1] Everett's On the Cam, pp. 182–183.

was fostered in college by a club for reading poetry, in which they were joined with three or four others. When the Cambridge Union entered its new building, and Lord Houghton delivered the address, this ,was part of a published letter :

Lord Houghton's beautiful reviving of those old days has in it something fragrant and sweet, and brings back old faces and old friendships very dear as life is drawing to its close. Yours, etc.   HENRY E. MANNING.

Imagine the friendships which must have grown up in days when Tennyson, Alford, Trench and Maurice belonged to the Union, and when a deputation, of which Arthur Hallam was one, was " sent from the Union of Cambridge to the Union of Oxford * * to assert the right of Mr. Shelley to be considered a greater poet than Lord Byron ;" [1] and was entertained at Oxford "by a young student of the name of Gladstone."

Goethe, who created the literature and perhaps led the thinking of Germany, and who speaks with the authority of a magnificent intellectual and social endowment, says of his university friends, " Without the external forms, which do so much mischief in universities, we represented a society bound together by circumstances and good feeling, which others might occasionally touch, but into which they could not intrude." [2]

There is in Cambridge University a society, the Apostles, "a strictly private club, and in no

[1] Cambridge Union Speeches, pp. 12, 13.
[2] Autobiography, p. 320.

way putting itself prominently forward,"[1] usually composed of thirteen members, of whom
"all had a certain fondness for literary and met-
aphysical pursuits in common;" who "did not
make any parade of mystery, or aim at notoriety
by any device to attract attention. * * did
not have special chambers for meeting," and
"did not attempt to throw any awful veil of
secrecy over their proceedings." It was known
that they "met to read essays and hold discussions, with occasional interludes of supper."
Their "immediate and tangible influence in the
University amounted to just nothing." Now it
may not be well that such a club should be permanent, all things considered; but if it is—and
there are some advantages in permanence—some
plan like the above would seem to be the true
one.

It may be urged that secret societies meet the
legitimate demand for ordinary general society,
by affording a common meeting-place for men
of different classes, and graduates. This is
partly true; but there is no demand here which
could not be met by open clubs. A large part
of it, also, is met by mixed society and by social
occasions incident to college life; when members of the faculty, for instance, entertain students who take their optionals or who are in
their divisions, as some of them do, the same or
greater benefits may be derived with none of the
evils. Officers of the college do not seem to
realize how greatly they might thus increase the
pleasure of the students, as well as their influence over them in every direction. In one

[1] Bristed's Five Years in an English University, pp.
157, 158.

aspect, the societies may express a demand for
something of the kind suggested by President
Porter, who says : " Is it desirable that public
parlors should be furnished, or places conven-
ient for rendezvous and conversation?" [1] and
adds, " an accessible and cheerful reading-room,
amply furnished with the best newspapers and
journals, should be esteemed a necessity, and if
it were made attractive and tasteful in its ap-
pointments, and supplied with retiring rooms
for conversation, and could also be rigidly controlled by the rules of gentlemanly etiquette,
would be a most desirable and useful agency in
the college community."

It is obvious that the societies supply such a
want most inadequately.   They are usually limited to a few ; and if they were more numerous,
society would still be divided into rigidly exclusive cliques, which could offer no hospitality to
one another or to strangers.   The University of
Leyden has a great central house, of three stories,
managed by the students, with reading-room,
parlors for conversation, and other students'
conveniences ; which is open to the whole University, and does much to unify the students.
Such an institution would perhaps meet the
want already noticed, of some place where graduates returning to the college might feel that
they were welcome and at home.   The University Club, lately established in this college, may
be regarded as a step in this direction ; but there
are several reasons why, as yet, it does not by
any means fill such a place.

. Looking at the societies as meeting a demand

[1] American Colleges, p. 196.

for club life, I do not believe this a legitimate demand in college, and not often elsewhere. The legitimate wants are sufficiently met by the college system and the natural associations growing out of it; while club life gives undue prominence to social and physical enjoyments, as such, and is not calculated for the true ends of college life. This principle given by President Porter applies equally here : " If college students are distributed in lodgings throughout the village or city they will form sets and associate in cliques, which, the more intimate and exclusive they are, are likely to become more narrowing, but they cannot partake of a general public life with its manifold cross and counter currents, its checks and counter checks, the influence of which upon the plastic minds of active minded and sagacious youth is liberalizing in an eminent degree." [1]   Of the student, " it is not desirable that he should be restricted to the uncertain chances and narrowing influences of a private and exclusive clique." Dr. Howard Crosby says of club life, in its relation to the family, " The secrecy of the college society renders it peculiarly adapted to be a rival to the family. Now a young man too easily learns the false and sad lesson that it is manly to slight domestic ties and substitute a species of club life in its place, and where that club-life takes on the fascinations of secrecy, the danger is greatly augmented." [2]   On this point may be

[1] American Colleges, pp. 187, 188.
[2] College Secret Societies, published by Ezra A. Cook, Chicago ; p. 33.

given the following letter, published recently in the *Boston Advertiser :*" [1]

The undersigned, members of the Hasty Pudding club living in Cambridge, Boston and neighborhood, taking a hearty interest in its welfare, and regarding its character as of no slight importance, have observed with regret the attempts now making to raise funds for the erection of a house for the club.   To provide the club with a house of its own, would be, in their judgment, likely to foster a mode of club life undesirable in itself, and inconsistent with the simple and pleasant traditions of the Hasty Pudding. They believe that such a change as would result from this innovation would prove injurious to the club,—by increasing the expenses of its members, and consequently limiting the range of selection, and making membership depend on other qualities than those of genuine good fellowship ; and, further, by exaggerating the importance of purely club interests, and thus promoting the tendency, at all times strong among undergraduates, to subordinate the real interests and objects of their college life to social pleasures and trivial occupations.

The undersigned, therefore, earnestly beg their fellow graduate members of the Hasty Pudding club to consider whether they wish to aid in carrying out a design which cannot but greatly change the long-established character of the club, and which will endanger both its pleasantness and its usefulness.

CHARLES F. DUNBAR,	C. E. NORTON,
JOHN C. GRAY,	G. H. PALMER,
J. B. GREENOUGH,	FRANCIS G. PEABODY,
E. W. GURNEY,	A. T. PERKINS,
A. S. HILL,	GEORGE PUTNAM,
ARCHIBALD M. HOWE,	H. W. PUTNAM,
H. HOWLAND,	J. B. THAYER,
C. L. JACKSON,	MOSES WILLIAMS, JR.
ARTHUR E. JONES,	

April 4, 1882.

These include the Dean and ten other members of the Harvard faculty.   It should, perhaps,

[1] Boston Daily Advertiser, April 10, 1882.

be added that the *Advertiser* of April 26th contained a reply from an active member of the club, and promised one from graduate members; but, up to June 2, no further communication on this subject had been printed in the *Advertiser*.

Student friendships, then, do not need secret societies. Great natural and healthy forces work in association and friendship which will secure all right ends without calling in the doubtful aid of secrecy and exclusiveness. Viewed as taking the place of general society, the societies are inadequate, besides being open to other objections; as promoting club life, they foster a demand which is not legitimate.

The discussion has thus far considered this system as social, because, on the whole, that is its most prominent feature, though particular societies may be chiefly literary or political.   The introduction to the catalogue of Psi Upsilon, from which some of Ex-Gov. Hawley's words have been quoted, dwells mainly on this.   Baird does the same. [1]   Prof. Coe, in his article on the Literary Societies of Yale, says that the secret societies were " the expression of a want long felt in the larger bodies; the want of *sociability.*[2] " Class societies flourished * * because they knew how to promote friendship and friendly sociability, whether they conferred intellectual and moral benefits or not."

[1] American College Fraternities, circ. p. 195.
[2] History of Yale College, p. 322.

CHAPTER III.

Wisdom is better than rubies.—*Solomon.*

The secret societies are claimed to be substitutes for the literary societies. On this view of the case, partly a true one, several things are obvious. The first is, that they are usually limited to a few, an objection which their advantages should be very great to atone for. Selectness and privacy, it may be said, give opportunity for free and sympathetic discussion and criticism. But this advantage must be largely overset by the usual combination of so many heterogeneous elements, the advantages of which can hardly be literary, whatever else they may be. The societies are generally—not always—somewhat political in character, and seek men prominent in various ways. Hence those who would make the strength of a literary society are usually scattered through several clubs, and mixed up with men of very small literary taste and sympathy. The spirit of these institutions tends strongly to become political or social; neither being at all favorable to a literary spirit. Still deeper objections are that secrecy and exclusiveness are hostile to the growth of the love of truth, which by its very nature is diffusive, and, like friendship, more vigorous in the open air than in the hot-house. Then, too, while a select circle has some literary advantages, they are not those of public debate. The latter give opportunity for those trials of intellectual strength which make the mind strong and active and ready, as athletic contests do the body. Before the Alumni meeting at the Yale commencement of 1873, Hon. William M. Evarts said that the great debating societies of Yale "furnished for the field for open and manly debate what could not be found in the small numbers and limited opportunities of the secret societies. They prepared the young man to withstand frowns and hisses as well as applause, and turned out men who could meet an adversary in debate without flinching. All this is wanting now, and cannot be supplied unless the old societies can be resurrected."[1] In the debating societies of Cambridge and Oxford, says George William Curtis, "the long illustrious list of noted and able Englishmen were trained, and in the only way that manly minds can be trained, by open, free, generous rivalry and collision."[2] Public audiences are needed, also, to develop the patriotism and public feeling which are among the best elements of debate, as well as its inspiration. Lieber declares that "publicity is indispensable to eloquence. No one speaks well in secret before a few."[3] "Truth for the world" is unconsciously the thought of the young orator, and well it may be; for at the fountain-heads of influence, among young men in school and college, these discussions often have immeasurable results. "A debate whether Pope or Wordsworth was the greater poet," said the *Spectator*, in reference to the Cambridge Union,[4] "whether

[1] Hartford Courant, June 26, 1873.
[2] Harper's Monthly, January, 1874.
[3] Civil Liberty, p. 134.
[4] Cambridge Union Speeches, pp. 59–60.

Greece or Rome had exercised the most beneficial influence on the world, whether Carlyle or
Mill were the truer teacher, has often, we feel no
doubt, done more to determine the future lives
of great men, and through them the future of
England, than hundreds of so-called ' practical '
debates in the House of Commons." There is a
further loss in the ignorance of parliamentary
law, to the study of which the nature of secret
societies is not often favorable. For these losses
a private literary club has some compensations;
but in the secret society system they are reduced
to a minimum.

That secret societies break up the literary societies, and do not merely supplement them, I
think is beyond question. Baird practically ad-
mits it.[1] "A radical change," says Professor
Tyler, of Amherst, " has come over the old literary societies in all the colleges, leaving them
little else than a name."[2] In 1845, the literary
societies of Amherst "had long been altogether
secondary in interest to the ' Greek Letter Fraternities,' which had in fact drawn their very life-
blood out of them ;"[3] and though the former still
survive, they are said to be half dying. Dr.
Howard Crosby says, " I believe that I am right
in asserting that in most of our colleges the literary societies (most important helps to the student in composition and oratory) have been utterly ruined, except as alumni centers, by the secret societies."[4] Secret societies are not allowed

[1] American College Fraternities, circ. p. 195.
[2] History of Amherst College, p. 316.
[3] Do., p. 314.
[4] College Secret Societies, published by Ezra A. Cook,
Chicago ; p. 35.

at Princeton, and the great literary societies are
flourishing; both secret, indeed, but as both are
purely literary, and membership is open to
every college man, the evils of secrecy are comparatively small.   " The rise of the new Greek
Letter Fraternities,'" also says Prof. Tyler, " has
obscured the light and glory of the old literary
societies in nearly all the colleges.   In Yale college, the Linonian and the Brothers, which, like
rival queens, reigned in the hearts of so many
generations of students, have thus been extin-
guished."   Ex-President Woolsey holds the
same opinion.   Mr. Evarts, in the speech above
referred to, "advocated the revival of the old
societies and the suppression of the foolish secret clubs which have supplanted them."   This
last is denied, however ; and Prof. Coe[2] names
several causes, as the rise of the athletic system,
the development of the curriculum, and a loss
of interest in public speaking.   Doubtless these
had some influence ; but no one of them, nor all
together, have been as potent as the secret societies.   This became evident when Linonia was
revived in '78.   The society started with a great
deal of enthusiasm ; but many of the best men
had their society interest centered elsewhere.
Less prominent men felt this, and could not continue to be cordially united with them, partly
because of the barriers between, partly because
they felt that Linonia was regarded as second-
rate.   The devotion and loyalty which are the
life of a society could not be developed.   Probably finding that two societies took up too much

[1] History of Amherst College, p. 630.
[2] History of Yale College, p. 322.

time, and caring more for others than for Linonia,
the society men also began to drop off. Another
reason, due especially to the class system, was
the peculiar feeling between classes. Instead of
being "the gala night of all the week,'" as in the
olden time, when all classes met "on a footing of
perfect equality, though the Seniors naturally
took the lead," all the under-class men felt themselves under the power of that peculiar bedevil-
ment emanating from a society man which piles
barriers mountain high above them, and makes
them, supposing themselves the objects of cold
and critical attention, hardly dare to open their
mouths. So they felt it was no place for them ;
the enthusiastic leaders of the movement had
raised up no successors, and for these and kindred reasons the society dwindled till its death.
Had its members thrown away their pins, and
made it the centre of their society life, I believe
Linonia would have been strong to-day. Whatever good the secret societies may have done,
the destruction of the literary societies, a very
serious loss, is chiefly due to them.

The value of literary societies is so generally
admitted that its discussion may be unnecessary ;
but as this college generation, unfortunately,
knows little of them, it may well be noticed.
Most apparent among their advantages is that
of training in public speaking. This is sometimes decried, as an accomplishment of an earlier and less civilized age ; but wrongly. Oratory is perhaps the noblest of arts. Neither De-
mosthenes nor Cicero belonged to an unculti-
vated age. Daniel Webster can hardly be rele-

---

[1] Four Years at Yale, p. 200.

gated to an uncivilized generation ; and England might never have seen the great Liberal victories of recent times had it not been for Mr. Gladstone's peerless eloquence. That the increase of printing and other causes have somewhat lessened the demand for public speaking may be true, but the time will never come when men will not demand the personal power of oratory, and be for it both wiser and better. One good campaign speaker will accomplish more than tons of printed speeches.

Public speaking is especially important under the constitutional forms of Anglican liberty. " A most important feature of Anglican publicity of legislative, judicial and of many of the common administrative transactions," says Lieber.[1] " Modern centralized absolutism has developed a system of writing and secrecy, and consequent formalism, abhorrent to free citizens who exist and feed upon the living word of liberty. Bureaucracy is founded upon writing, liberty on the breathing word. * * * I do not believe that a high degree of liberty can be imagined without widely pervading orality." " If civil liberty demands representative legislative bodies, which it assuredly does, these bodies have no meaning without exchange and mutual modification of ideas, without debate, and actual debate requires the spoken word. I consider it an evil hour, not only for eloquence, but for liberty itself, when our Senate first permitted one of its members to read his speeches, on account of some infirmity. The true principle has now been abandoned," in Congress. Speaking

[1] Civil Liberty, pp. 128, 129, 134.

is a large part, also, of two out of the three great
professions. Public speaking, therefore, is in
demand, and will be; at the bar, in the pulpit,
on the platform, in the carrying on of government, on a thousand occasions of public life.

Kindred with these advantages is that of learning parliamentary law, which cannot well be
mastered except by practice; and with which, in
a country of constitutional forms, every freeman, above all, every educated freeman, who is
always likely to be a public man, ought to be
familiar. Of this the athletic meetings teach
little or nothing, though the case is not always
as bad as when the president of Yale's leading
athletic club dismissed a meeting with the remark, "I say, fellows, let's adjourn!"

The public college life which was one of their
great advantages has not disappeared with the
literary societies; to a large extent it has gath-
ered around the athletic system, and though it is
now probably carried too far, it has features of
considerable value. It interests many men
whom a literary system would not, it forms a
more general bond of union between the students,
and its inter-collegiate relations give it a wider
scope; each college struggling for the supremacy in athletics almost as vigorously as ever
Athens or Sparta did for the political supremacy. But literary societies would claim the allegiance of many—and these often the more
thoughtful—men when athletics do not and can
not; and there is also a large part of the year
when athletics are quiescent. Another point
may be made here, from the *Pall Mall Gazette*,
also referring to the Cambridge Union:[1] "The

[1] Cambridge Union Speeches, pp. 71, 72.

general, seducing, and ultimately destructive temptation to youth is the animal temptation— the temptation to enjoy early life in the pursuit of the coarsest and simplest gratifications, whether innocent or the reverse. * * Every student who turns from the wine-party, or the card-table, or the hunt, aye, or the cricket-field, or the river, to study a speech for the Union, or to make himself master of the arguments of others there, is exchanging a worse for a better thing, *as the general rule.* Exceptions there may be in abundance, but such is the law. On this principle, as on a rock, these debating societies rest, and must continue to rest until either some better substitute is invented, or the lower part of our nature establishes a recognized supremacy over the higher. But he would greatly understate their case who should simply rest it here."

Beyond the value of the information attained and the principles taught, important as these are, there is a further advantage, perhaps beyond all others. This is the intellectual vivifying and broadening and clearing which comes of the influence of mind over mind, and which few things effect as well as a good discussion. This can often be exerted far more powerfully by a fellow student than by an instructor; the boy is sent to school, and the school-boys educate him. The instructor is in a different sphere of thought, so far away from his pupils, often, that they catch no inspiration from him; while from a vigorous, progressive mind, working along the same lines with themselves, they often receive unmeasured impulses to like vigor and progress. So said Lord Houghton;[1] "the great

[1] Cambridge Union Speeches, p. 18.

gain * * is in the fair conflict of intel-
lects; it is in the meeting of man and man, of
mind and mind." The *Spectator*, also:[1] "Without the 'mere talk' of young men's theoretical
discussions, the collision of taste with taste, of
intellect with intellect, of conscience with conscience, of spirit with spirit, the characters of the
best men in the nation would scarcely come to
the birth at all." Those who witnessed the recent attempt to revive Linonia, at Yale, will re-
member the interest taken by many prominent
graduates, and their strong testimony to the
value of the literary societies. "Mr. Evarts," said
an editorial in the *Hartford Courant*, containing
the speech by him mentioned above, " who has
few equals and no superiors as a ready thinker
and talker, attributes no small degree of his
great success to the training of these societies;
and the same may be said of the ablest men who
have been graduated from Yale during the last
century." At Linonia's centennial, in 1853, Mr.
Evarts said in his oration: "I speak but the
common sentiment of the graduates and friends
of Yale college, and of all others who have had
occasion to compare the system of education
here, and its results, with the methods of other
universities, when I attribute no small share of
the permanent hold upon the confidence and respect of the whole country, which this university
has ever retained, to the influence of these great
literary societies; when I ascribe to the impulse
and the bent given to young minds in their
arena, no trivial portion of the service which in
every province of public activity the scholars of

[1] Cambridge Union Speeches, pp. 54-55.

this discipline have rendered to their generation."

It may be worthy of notice that while the advantages of literary societies much outweigh
their evils, some of these must be admitted.
They may trench somewhat upon the regular
studies; yet not often seriously. The best
speakers are very generally the best students.
Lord Houghton, in the address already referred
to, spoke of the time when Tennyson, Hallam,
Trench, Alford, Spedding, Merivale, Kemble,
Kinglake, Maurice, were at Cambridge, saying,
" Of these men, all, I believe, were members of
the Cambridge Union society, and most of them
active participants in its debates,'" and met this
very objection by adding, " The majority of these
men won your highest honors, and at the same
time were the best speakers in the Union."
Literary societies may sometimes encourage
superficiality ; but if there is anything which
will leave the ordinary man with a more pro-
found respect for the opinions of others, and
a deeper sense of how little he knows, than
a good discussion, it is rarely found. The
Spectator may here be quoted again :[2] " Debating societies for young men are not, properly speaking, schools of loquacity at all. There
is an age—the university age—when adequate
speech on the various motives and ends of life
becomes something altogether beyond mere
speech, the natural work, the appropriate action, the characteristic energy of the mind—and
when there is every reason for aiding this ex-

[1] Cambridge Union Speeches, p. 11.
[2] Do., pp. 54, 59.

pressive crystallization of thought and feeling;
*   *   an age at which theoretical discussions
ought to be, if they are not, the very means of
life and growth, when it is as silly to call such
discussions mere talk, as it is in later life to call
a cabinet council " such.   " This is not talk, it is
preparation for action, it is the stringing up and
organization of intellectual energy, it is intellectual volition."

Some value is claimed for the secret societies,
particularly under the class system, as raising
scholarship by exciting emulation.   Not dwell-
ing now on the important truth that the desire
to beat, or to win position, is not the true foundation of scholarship, which knows far nobler
ends : taking into account the dropping off in
the later years of the course, and the general
society influence, it is very doubtful if the final
result would show much gain.   " We regard
their influence as unfavorable upon the pre-
scribed course of study,"[1] says a college President.   " College secret societies interfere with a
faithful course of study," says Dr. Crosby.[2]   " I
always found the best students were those who
either kept out of the secret societies, or who
entered very slightly into their operations."

With the class system, especially, the general
effect of the societies upon college thought is de-
pressing.   This cast-iron system, with its silence,
its repression, its apparent spirit of criticizing
men, is fatal to the spirit of freedom and progress which is the spring of enthusiasm, and of
that buoyant intellectual life which comes forth

[1] Hitchcock's Reminiscences of Amherst College, p. 323.
[2] College Secret Societies, as above : p. 34.

sparkling in poetry or surging in oratory. Un-
reality, fascinating mystery, an eager struggle
for three years, and silent exclusion with its
consequent bitterness, make no soil for poetry
or eloquence or scholarship or letters.

Considered from the intellectual standpoint,
therefore, the secret societies do not fill the place
of the literary societies. For the destruction of
the latter they are chiefly responsible, and in
this destruction there have been lost educational
institutions of great value. The societies do not
help scholarship, on the whole, and they lie like
a heavy weight on the young intellectual life of
the college, repressing hope and enthusiasm, and
taking away the liberty out of which arises
thought and " oratory—the æsthetics of liberty."

CHAPTER IV.

POLITICAL RELATIONS.

Of old sat Freedom on the heights,
　The thunders breaking at her feet:
Above her shook the starry lights:
　She heard the torrents meet.

—Tennyson.

The societies may be political, or they may not. They may first be considered as political.

Under a despotism, political secret societies may furnish the only means whereby the Spirit of freedom can be kept alive, or resistance to tyranny maintained. Where the freedom of the press and the right of association do not exist, as in Russia, they seem almost a necessary agency for organization and for the promulgation of ideas. They probably had a great influence in disseminating the ideas and influences which led to the European revolutions of this century. They were "the secret conventicles of independent thought."[1] The Carbonari and the Young Italy, of which the latter was the creation of Mazzini's genius for the liberation of Italy, "kept alive for half a century, by their secret meetings and their secret correspondence, the spirit of resistance to foreign domination."[2] Yet even here, for reasons which will appear, they are probably admissible only as a last resort; and it has been noticed that England and

[1] Frost's Secret Societies of the European Revolution, Vol. I, p. 304.
[2] Do., Vol. II, p. 199.

Switzerland, countries which have won and kept more freedom than any others in Europe, have made least use of such agencies. Open agitation, as explained in passages already quoted from Lieber, is the method of Anglican liberty, whose freedom is the most perfect known.

The circumstances which would justify a revolution would also justify and usually necessitate secret organization. The object could hardly be reached in any other way. When the government was weak, again, some private organization might be needed for mutual protection, like the citizens' Vigilance Committee of San Francisco, in the old days of violence in that city. Such organizations, says Lieber, "are generally and necessarily for a time secret societies."[1] But plainly both of these are exceptional cases, like those which warrant the suspension of the writ of habeas corpus.

In free countries the case is quite different.

1. The multiplying of parties tends to disunion and bitterness. Says Burke, the "artificial division of mankind, into separate societies, is a perpetual source in itself of hatred and dissension among them."[2] Secrecy and exclusiveness much strengthen these effects. There is a constant jealousy and distrust, which easily ripens into bitter animosity.

2. In relation to the general government, they tend to exalt society over public allegiance, and to diminish public spirit. Their peculiar claims are calculated to weaken the public attachment. Says President Fairchild, of Oberlin,[3] "Every

[1] Political Ethics, 2d edition, Vol. II, p. 195.
[2] Works, Vol. I, p. 22.
[3] Moral Philosophy, p. 271.

4

organization, political or social, which tends to clannishness, weakens the common interest, and diminishes the proper national feeling, is inconsistent with the highest patriotism. Secret political and social organizations, as existing in this and other lands, seem to be of this nature. They tend to disorganize society, to sunder the ties upon which national unity depends."

3. Parties properly represent principles, not men; men only as they stand for principles. All parties easily forget this, but where they do not stand on public platforms, as secret societies do not, the tendency is very strong for them to become cliques, struggling only for power. The committee of the New York Senate, on Masonry, said in their report, "The opposers of Masonry at the West entertain no doubt that the institution was originally intended, and is now kept up, for the sole purpose of securing to its members, unjust advantages over their fellow-citizens, in the various concerns of life, but chiefly with the view of facilitating their acquisition of political power."[1]

4. Secret societies are exposed to a further special danger, that of intrigue and corruption. At the time of the Morgan excitement, Mr. Colden, ex-Mayor of New York, who had been "elevated to the highest honors of Masonry," and was "a citizen highly respected for his talents and character," wrote a letter giving his reasons for opposing Masonry, and among others mentioned "the peculiar adaptedness of Masonry to purposes of political intrigue and corruption."[2]

[1] Report in Vol. 91, of College Pamphlets, Yale Library, p. 14.
[2] Do., do., p. 21.

5. Political secret societies dispel the confidence essential to the stability of government. They are a perversion of the caucus principle, itself probably legitimate within certain limits, though doubtless often abused. "Confidence is indispensable for the government of free countries—it is the soul of loyalty in jealous freemen," says Lieber.[1] "This necessary influence is two-fold—confidence in the government, and confidence of society in itself. It is with reference to the latter that secret political societies in free countries are essentially injurious to all liberty." The committee already referred to said in their report that the people were jealous of combinations "for purposes either unknown or known to affect improperly, the even and healthful current of our political affairs," and proposed to withhold "political support from all its members indiscriminately, until they shall sunder their obligations to that institution (Masonry) and to each other, and return with us upon equal footing into the social compact."[2]

6. "All secret associations," says Edward Everett, "particularly all such as resort to the aid of secret oaths, are peculiarly at war with the genius of a republican government." "They are intrinsically hostile to liberty," says Lieber.[3] "They are, as all secret societies must inherently be, submissive to secret superior will and decision,—a great danger in politics,—and unjust to the rest of the citizens, by deciding on public measures and men without the trial of public discussion, and by bringing the influence of a

[1] Civil Liberty, p. 135.
[2] Report as above, p. 12.
[3] Civil Liberty, pp. 128, 135.

secretly united body to bear on the decision or election. Secret societies in free countries are cancers against which history teaches us that men who value their freedom ought to guard themselves most attentively." The expounder of our Constitution, Daniel Webster, asserts that "All secret associations, the members of which take upon themselves extraordinary obligations to one another and are bound together by secret oaths, are naturally sources of jealousy and just alarm to others, are especially unfavorable to harmony and mutual confidence among men living together under popular institutions, and are dangerous to the general cause of civil liberty and good government."

The societies may not be political. This would much better the case; but many of the above objections would still hold. While maintaining secrecy, they must still have political significance. It is not known that they are not political; hence they still create dissension and dispel confidence. Their members are often supposed to be backed by the organization, and therefore have precisely the same influence as if they were, sometimes, perhaps, without knowing it. There is also a strong tendency within the society itself to exert its latent power in politics, particularly at certain crises. These last points were illustrated at the time of the Morgan excitement. It is doubtful if Masonry was ever a political society in this country, though it was made such in Mexico. Yet it had exerted so much political influence, in one way and another, as to cause the formation of a national party against it, on such grounds as this, that while

Masonry comprised one-ninth of the voting population of the State of New York, its members held three-fourths of the offices. If it had not become political, it was nevertheless regarded as such. Many of the above objections, therefore, apply to non-political societies, though not to the same degree.

The societies may be viewed as that union of the political and social called an aristocracy, and this is probably their truest aspect. Secrecy, exclusiveness, and badges are the expression of an aristocratic spirit. In the letter already mentioned, Ex-Mayor Colden said, " Foreigners must think we are not less fond 'of the show and trapping, and titles of aristocracy and royalty, than any other people, when they see that we are so eager to adopt them, in the only way tolerated by our political institutions."[1] Their strength and weakness is almost exactly that of an aristocracy. They generally seem to aim at prestige and power by the choice of prominent men. They "would of course have little prestige," says President Hitchcock, of Amherst, "were they not strongly exclusive, so as in fact to leave out a majority of the students, nor unless those selected embraced the élite as to scholarship."[2] " Everything for the few, nothing for the many," is an aristocracy, the world over; and that is the essential principle of these societies. Plainly this is true as to social and literary advantages; and, for reasons already given, it is often true politically.

In this land and age, itself in one aspect a glorious refutation of aristocratic principles, it

[1] Report as above, p. 21–22.
[2] Reminiscences of Amherst College, p. 320.

can hardly be necessary to dwell on the larger
truths of republicanism, or the objections to
aristocracy. Its social aspect has been already
considered; I only add here that, like every aristocracy, it has its advantages, sometimes of a
very noble kind. That is a poor idea of an aristocracy which limits these to food and clothing,
houses and carriages. But much nobler things
may be misused, as already explained. The
"glorious good-fellowship" of college would
be far more glorious and much more of a real
fellowship, to say nothing of its goodness, without the aristocratic element; which means selfishness, in plain English, and which really does
not belong to it at all. The nobler spirits are
united in a natural aristocracy, which needs no
external forms; and their due influence classmates are ready and glad to recognize. "Within
the ethnical circle of good society," writes
Emerson, "there is a narrower and higher circle,
concentration of its light, and flower of courtesy,
to which there is always a tacit appeal of pride
and reference, as to its inner and imperial
court, the parliament of love and chivalry."[1]
Politically, aristocracy means what John Stuart
Mill calls "the monster evil—the over-ruling
influence of oligarchy,"[2] establishing an oppression more or less grievous. The kind of
oppression here is what Lieber means when he
says, "Oppression does not come from government or official bodies alone. The worst oppression is of a social character, or by a multitude."[3]

[1] Essays, 2d series, p. 160.
[2] Dissertations and Discussions, Vol. IV, p. 39.
[3] Civil Liberty, p. 88.

As aristocracies, these societies are an anachronism. They abandon the free and progressive ideas of modern civilization, and go back to the narrow and selfish and unprogressive systems of mediæval times.

CHAPTER V.

POLITICAL INFLUENCE.

—Where's the manly spirit
Of the true-hearted and the unshackled gone?
Sons of old freemen, do we but inherit
Their names alone?

— Whittier.

These political principles hold in college, as elsewhere, and work the same effects, though with some modifications. Here also, as parties, the societies tend to dispel confidence, to sow dissension, and to undermine republican principles; as aristocracies, they exalt the few at the expense of the many, by giving them undue political influence and by creating exclusive cliques which monopolize social and literary advantages.

The relation between classes under the class system is one of its great objections. The fact that the odious word "supe" is one of the most familiar in the Yale undergraduate vocabulary, tells the whole story. Freshmen ordinarily do not understand this great factor in college life, but gradually they begin to feel its mysterious power, and by the spring of Junior year men hardly dare "to say their souls are their own," as the current phrase runs. So subtle is this influence that it often has complete mastery, though one who had not felt its power would not suspect it. It is omnipresent, making itself felt in the smallest details. It was once reported in Yale and generally believed that a prominent disappointed candidate said that he had bought

three new suits of clothes that spring, to "im-
prove his chances." If a man subscribes well to
college athletics, it will be hinted that he is
"suping;" and sometimes, probably, he is. A
man dares not congratulate his society friend in
the upper classes on their successes; if he does,
he will be "suping."

These things are only incidents in a system of
domination over the minds of men which is abhorrent to the spirit of freedom. Class societies
"lead younger students," says a prominent graduate, "to adapt their manners and, to some
extent, their life to the approbation of those in
higher classes, whom they look upon as likely
to be influential in their behalf, instead of being
governed by elevated principles and a high sense
of honor." Undoubtedly this repression has
some good effects, as urged by Baird, who brings
forward the salutary discipline often exercised
by the societies; but there are some good
things pertaining to every tyranny. Public
sentiment, too, among a community including so many men of upright character as a
college does, considerably limits this evil, many
men being driven to take the opposite extreme
of independent conduct, as well explained in
the leading article of the *Yale Literary Magazine*
for May, 1882 : yet few communities are capable
of a more universal and servile subjection of
opinion, for the time being, than a college community. With all its limitations, there are few
men whom this influence does not warp somewhat from the true ; and it is still enough to fill
the soul with righteous hatred of all such domination over human freedom.

The societies embitter factions. Parties, indeed, will always exist; and Baird draws a picture of a scene in one of the old literary societies, with the constitution flying out of the window and the chairman after it. No doubt there might be occasional bad feeling under any system; but it could come out in ways far healthier and better for the students than with the suppressed bitterness and jealousy incident to the secret system. It is the difference between bad blood breaking out on the surface, or remaining in the system; of which the former may look worse, but is far better for health and soundness. Says a college President,[1] "Their general effect is to sow dissensions and produce factions in a degree in which they were never known to exist here before, and so as to render the elections of the several societies scenes of most unhappy division." Another President,[2] "They break the college into parties, produce jealousies, contentions and a difficulty of promoting any object of general utility among the students." President Robinson, of Brown, "They foster a spirit of clannishness and lead to the formation of cliques in the classes, interfering with the class feeling, and sometimes destroying utterly the *esprit de corps* which it is so desirable for every class to cherish."[3] This last would not be true to the same degree under a class system; yet a graduate says that in Yale they "stimulate petty intrigue," and "give

[1] Hitchcock's Reminiscences of Amherst, p. 323.
[2] Do., do., p. 325.
[3] Report to the Corporation of Brown University, June, 1876; p. 16.

opportunity for slights in the bestowment of students' honors, which embitter the remainder of college life, and, in some cases, of after years." "Prominent among" the evils with which "such societies may be, and sometimes are, attended," President Porter mentions "the fostering of an intriguing and political spirit, which is incongruous with the general tendencies of college life toward justice and generosity ; and the division of the community and the classes into hostile factions."[1] "I am confident," says President Hitchcock, however, "that the evils feared from them have much diminished."[2] In Yale, also, many of them have disappeared with the giving up of the Wooden Spoon, and of coalitions between the Junior societies, with the abolition of the societies of the two lower classes and the giving up of class elections for the biweekly papers; though the method of appointment by the editors gives the latter so much power as to involve some of the same objections. Of late years, therefore, there has been a considerable progress in Yale toward a more wholesome and generous public life ; yet a straw occasionally shows that there is a wind still blowing the wrong way. The Senior neutrals sometimes hold a private caucus before the election of class committees, in which the ticket is so arranged as to exclude every society man ; a singular proceeding, when it is remembered that the society men are presumably the best and most popular men of the class. I need not dwell on the undercurrent of feeling shown by such a fact.

[1] American Colleges, p. 195.
[2] Reminiscences of Amherst College, p. 325.

When allowed at Harvard, the societies created such feeling that in one instance the Seniors could not or would not arrange for their class day, and the Faculty were obliged to get up some sort of a programme for the occasion. It may be true, as Baird says, that the societies do not introduce politics; but they do introduce into them unnecessary elements of bitterness.

As to direct outward influence on undergraduate interests, matters are probably about evenly balanced. Some years athletics have doubtless suffered seriously, either from society men's presuming on their position to break training rules, or from their indifference to college interests after themselves attaining the coveted honors, or from favoritism in management, or from a general lack of patriotism. It is also said, and probably with some truth, that the society influence is unfair with respect to the choice of men for various positions, as on the papers or the Glee Club. But these evils are much checked by honor and the pressure of public sentiment; and also largely balanced by the zeal aroused by society ambition and by society rivalries.

The real mischief, however, lies deeper; in the principles and methods, and their influence, which is against that public discussion of men and measures which is so vital to civil liberty. This, in case of a political society, has been already explained. Under the class system, it is felt in reference to the system itself. Its supporters will have no discussion of it; hence its real nature and tendencies are not understood. Its effects are not known. Whole classes may and often do feel themselves bitterly galled by their subjection to it; but no man dares to open

his mouth. It is also specially felt in reference
to public men and measures. It frequently
shields those who hold public offices from mer-
ited criticism. It prevents large numbers of
men from speaking and voting independently
on public measures. The Junior class, particularly, feels itself almost literally bound hand and
foot, so far as any public action is concerned.
The freedom of university meetings is very much
impaired by this influence. Devotion to the society also is likely to overshadow regard for the
college, so that men do not feel a hearty devotion
to college interests, as a quotation from a college
President has already suggested. College honors come to be valued not as tokens and rewards
of college patriotism, but as stepping-stones or
trophies for a society. The tendency is for men
to work in athletics not for the honor of the college, but to get into a society; which puts the
thing on a false foundation, for no one would
admit for a moment that such was his real motive. So, whether organizations are managed
in the society interest or not, it is very often believed that they are, which, as already explained,
is fatal to confidence and harmony. All secret
societies tend very strongly to favoritism ; and
" how utterly unjust and subversive of the best
interests of the State " this is, it needs not those
letters of Washington to which Lieber refers to
show.[1]

Societies are an annoying and hampering influence in the relations between the general body
of students and the Faculty. The society con-
nections of instructors lie directly athwart the

[1] Political Ethics, 2d edition, Vol. II, p. 29.,

path of that progress whereby the students of the larger colleges are outgrowing the school-boy notion of what these relations must be, and coming nearer to the true relation of pupil and master. To the imagination of the undergraduate aspirant, these instructors seem to be invested with all of the mysterious society power, and consequently capable of about as much sympathy and enthusiasm as an iceberg. He often regards them as working secretly to advance their own organization. Doubtless the student sometimes gains from the society ambition inspired by these relations; but he generally loses more in other ways than he gains here. Even when further experience modifies his views of the matter, he cannot help feeling that such officers are identified with extra-college interests, or that they are united with a particular part of the students in a way which threatens injustice and certainly involves loss of sympathy for the rest. What has been said about the society influence on college patriotism and about favoritism may sometimes apply here with regard to marks and college honors; but probably much less often, to men of such character as college officers usually are, than undergraduates suppose. The effects above mentioned are largely due to the secrecy.

It may be noticed that there is a question as to whether society considerations should enter into the choice of college officers, on either side. This would depend on the importance attached to the society influence, for good or evil. Clearly no society, as such, ought to exert an atom of political influence for or against a candidate. Officers who had never joined the societies would be free to act more impartially, but they could not understand as well the nature of the institutions with which they had to deal. Society men, on the other hand, could hardly avoid being influenced somewhat by considerations of party fealty; and, while maintaining such reserve as at Yale, they would not be in a favorable position to understand or measure the society influence on the great body of students and graduates, or to deal adequately with questions of reform. The general principle would seem to be that society considerations ought to be kept very subordinate, if admitted at all; but there are reasons which might make them worthy of serious attention.

Very important is the bearing of this question on the college patriotism of graduates, the feeling which men have for *Alma Mater*. Societies may bind men's affections, but these tend to center in the society, not in the college. The literary societies sometimes trenched on the college province, but not as the secret societies do. The latter may bring men back to Commencement, but when there the tendency is to exalt the society much above its true place, as compared with the college. Graduates are also led to give their money in ways less profitable than might be. Can any man doubt that if the thousands of dollars which have gone into the society halls of this institution had gone into the buildings of literary societies, for instance, they would have done far more good? A graduate says: There is "hardly a doubt but that the buildings have, in every instance, been erected by the contributions of graduates of the college who were members of the societies while they were here. There are four such buildings. One of them is said to have cost more than $40,000." Proportionate expenditures for the others would raise the total to at least a hundred thousand dollars. Suppose it to be admitted, for the moment, that the advantages of secret societies do on the whole outweigh their evils; yet is it not clear that the latter, on the whole, are so serious as to make the return for the outlay a very small one, so far as the undergraduates are concerned? If, then, it be further admitted that the graduates are to some extent building club-houses for themselves, which helps the case for the societies in this respect: even then does it not appear that the same sums could be given to the college for much better purposes? But if, still holding the latter supposition, we take what is probably the true view, that the evils do outweigh the advantages, and the principle is a wrong one, such investments must appear to be very seriously mistaken indeed.

Neutrals, on the other hand, must be much alienated, particularly under such a class system as that in Yale. There is something terrible about the silent exclusion, stern and cold as death, and as hopeless, by which they are left out of what they believe the controlling powers of the college. A recent graduate of an Eastern college says of one society in his college, "Whatever it may have intended to be in its origin, it has certainly grown into a political brotherhood with branches extending in many directions." In certain cities " the members pull together in every way they can; and I might give startling instances of how they favor one another in places and ways that seem beyond their reach.

They are not many but are enough when a unit to control college politics. They struck in years ago to secure control of the Faculty and they have it. They might have more representatives there, but do not wish it, because that would be a concentration of power which would weaken the forces for other fields of operation." This is not quoted to endorse its statements, as true of the system generally or of any particular society, but to show how some neutrals regard the societies. This must weaken college patriotism. " I am quite certain that the mass of the students feel less interest in the prosperity of the University than they were wont to do," writes an old graduate of Yale. In such matters men are very much influenced, often unconsciously, by their feelings and impressions; and among these, few are so deep and lasting as those caused by a social slight, or by being regarded or treated as inferior. That the secret system in college involves a systematic treatment of this kind is clear; though men do not realize it, because it happens to be the custom to inflict it on one side, and to put up with it on the other. This considerably modifies the effect but it does not remove it. Nor must this be taken to mean that the alumni of Yale are not substantially loyal to her. The subscriptions for the athletic grounds and the enthusiasm of the alumni associations would show that they are ; but it seems certain that this is in spite of the secret system, not because of it. It is said that alumni of the college have refused to send their sons to Yale because of the secret society system there domi-

5

nant; and that thousands of dollars of endowment are withheld from the college for the same
reason.

The unfavorable effect on college thought, already noticed, is largely explained by these
political influences.   Thought has its roots deep
in the political structure of society, and finds in
freedom its native soil.   The Greek and Roman
republics, for instance, gave the world immortal
literatures; but the rival despotisms of the East
produced little or nothing of value.   Secret societies cramp college thought, by taking away
the spontaneity and inspiration of freedom.

Nor are such influences calculated to form the
highest public character.   I believe that in most
cases it does require a sacrifice of manliness and
independence to join a society whose customs
and requirements are secret.   The candidate is
committing himself to the control of those who
have no rightful authority over him, to methods
which he does not know, for objects which he
does not know; and the sacrifice is in principle
the same, it will be seen, quite irrespectively of
what these really are.   The spirit and methods
of a secret system, as already discussed, are
essentially opposed to the development of a vigorous and independent type of character.   Says
John Stuart Mill,[1] speaking of the ballot as a
means of concealment, " If it be one of the par-
amount objects of national education to foster
courage and public spirit, it is high time now
that people should be taught the duty of asserting and acting openly on their opinions.   Disguise in all its forms is a badge of slavery."

[1] Dissertations and Discussions, Vol. IV, p. 46.

The society may be a despotism, itself under secret superior control. It often claims allegiance for life, a despotic principle which progressive government left behind long ago. Part of the unwritten law of Masonry, for example, is, " That obedience to Masonic law and authority, being voluntarily assumed, is of perpetual obligation, and can only be divested by the sanction of the supreme government in Masonry."[1] Though the voluntary nature of the contract lends some plausibility to this claim, yet its artificial character and the ignorance on the part of the candidate of what his contract really is make his right of resignation as complete as in other organizations, or even more so. There would probably be an obligation, however, to keep the secrets, as after belonging to a party of any kind.

It is one of the glories of a college to make its sons ready to enter on the high duties and honors of public life. In this training, one great element is the imparting of a generous public spirit. But in this the influence of the societies is not a help, but a hindrance. "They lead,"[2] says President Robinson, of Brown, "in the management of class affairs, to habits of intrigue and to the practice of the low arts of the politician. Combinations and bargains are often made to secure or defeat the election of candidates for parts in the exercises of class day, at the end of the college course, which are wholly inconsistent with the disingenuousness of youth

[1] American Pamphlets, Yale Library, Vol. 3, Constitution of Grand Lodge of New York, p. 21.
[2] Report as above, p. 16.

and scholars." If the public honors of graduates, however, are due to their knowledge of
politicians' arts acquired under the pressure of
this system, they are not honorable, either to
them or to the college. These considerations
do not now have as much force in Yale as they
once did, probably; but apart from particular
manifestations of it, the general truth remains
that the secret society is at variance with true
public spirit. The tendency of a secret system
is to rear up a generation of politicians, not of
statesmen.

Political secret societies, therefore, are open
to grave objections; and, if not political, many
of these still hold. They are still aristocracies,
and their public influence has many hurtful elements, both among students and graduates.

CHAPTER VI.

MORAL VALUE.

Love Virtue, she alone is free.—*Milton.*

Moral obligation is based in the nature of God, and all moral questions may therefore be included under the general head of religion. Yet morality may be considered independently of its religious ground; and the influence of a system on certain principles is to some extent a distinct question from its influence on the relation to God in which they are based, and still more distinct from its influence on the institution which maintains them, in this case the church of Christ. Some considerations, therefore, may properly be given as to the general moral influence of the societies.

The societies do some good in developing those qualities which make men capable of successful organized effort. Their requirements train men to the invaluable habit of faithfulness; and the maintenance of their secrecy develops fidelity and trustworthiness. They also teach men how to unite and live with their fellows in social relations, and how to apply their united energies in continued effort. All of this is valuable; but the greater part of it is incidental to any organization, and can be learned as well from membership of a base ball nine, or any other live association.

The societies may establish and maintain a certain standard of honor. Says ex-Governor Hawley, as already quoted, "There is a great positive value in the cordial, mutual pledges, of confidence, assistance, trust, encouragement, equality, fidelity, and honor." [1]   This value may be in cultivating the sense of honor, which is a binding force in society, and, if rightly defined as "a fine sense of justice," is most worthy of cultivation. An instinctive aversion to anything really dishonorable is one element of true character. But the law of honor has an almost invariable tendency to become simply a law of custom, so that when the code prescribes a duel, the man of honor will always fight. In his lectures to the Yale Seniors, President Porter says, [2] "The law of honor may be in conflict with the law of duty and the law of God." The imminent danger in cultivating this is that it may come to overshadow the great truths by which men should live. "The *law of honor*," says Dr. Paley, quoted by President Dwight, [3] "is a system of rules, constructed by people of fashion, and calculated to facilitate their intercourse with one another, and for no other purpose. Consequently it forbids nothing, but what tends to incommode this intercourse. Accordingly, it allows profaneness and impiety in every form." The true law of life is not the law of honor nor even the law of duty alone, but the Christian law of love, which at once transcends and includes them both. Lieber's remark has special force here: "No moral phenomenon is more common than that the more compact an association becomes, the more its members are apt, be it by the common *esprit de corps* or by an errone-

[1] Psi Upsilon Catalogue, p. xi.
[2] I quote from memory.
[3] Sermons, Vol. I, p. 424.

ous feeling of honor, to value the interest of the association higher than any other, and sometimes, as has but too frequently happened, to end in adopting a moral code or standard of their own, to be judged of only by the promotion' of the interests of that association." [1]

Good is sometimes done, particularly in the colleges, through the influence of men of strong moral character over their fellows in a society ; but, as a general thing, the good men are hurt more than the bad men are helped. This point will be further considered in another connection.

It is claimed that the fraternity watches over and reclaims from wrong-doing its weaker members, particularly in the colleges. Without doubt, some good is done in this way ; but, after deducting the amount due to other relations, particularly the close bonds of college life, the gain due to the fraternity would probably not be very large. Then, too, the assistance is limited by artificial society lines, which operate to withdraw it from some who would otherwise receive it.

One of the great arguments put forth by those who defend the societies is the benevolence which they practice, to which some organizations devote large sums of money. Two things are to be said here : In the first place, it is a partial benevolence. It limits its kindness to members of its own clan, and pays no heed to others. It is true that society teaching often inculcates universal benevolence ; but these admonitions are practically nullified by the exclusive

---

[1] Political Ethics, 2d edition, Vol. II, p. 197.

spirit of most orders, so far as the society influence is concerned, and they do not result in extending to uninitiated persons, or to their families, those cash payments which constitute the claim to benevolence. Such benevolence would have left the man who fell among thieves to die by the roadside, unless he also had been a Samaritan. It is exactly that kind of benevolence spoken of in the Sermon on the Mount, for which our Lord expressly substitutes a larger and more unselfish benevolence. It is true that there are natural ties which to some extent direct all benevolence; but secret societies pervert this truth, as they do so many others. The trouble is that they institute an artificial benevolence which has no legitimate place, and consequently infringes either on the natural ties, or on the claims arising from the universal brotherhood of man. For instance, a stranger is hurt on the street; men help him a little, perhaps, until he makes some sign, when the members of his society instantly are ready to give him all possible relief; which last is very well, but it is hard to see why they should wait for the sign.

Secondly, this benevolence is not properly benevolence at all. It cannot be called benevolence when men help one another because they expect to be helped in return. The real principle is not benevolence, but mutual insurance. It may be all right to institute mutual insurance, but it is not benevolence. This is clearly shown by the fact that members of these societies generally forfeit their claims to assistance by failing to meet their dues, the investments of years being sometimes wholly lost in this way. Some real benevolence there is, no doubt, incidentally, but it cannot be claimed on this ground that the associations are essentially benevolent, any more than a railroad corporation is because it occasionally helps a poor employé. The Supreme Court of Maine, says a quotation from the Boston *Journal*, has declared that "a Masonic lodge is not a charitable or benevolent institution, and has decided that its real and personal estate is subject to taxation like other property."

Viewed as a plan of insurance, even, this can hardly be called a good economical system. In 1871, a revenue of $3,000,000 was claimed by one association, and the sum spent for relief was $800,000. A report of the Grand Lodge of New York for 1881 gives total receipts, $83,556.55; charity, $405. The Grand Lodge of Massachusetts reports for last year, total receipts $107,246.03; for charity and funeral expenses, $1,563.79. To be sure, it may be said that the balance is expended for other good objects; but these have been separately discussed, and, at all events, must be balanced against a considerable expenditure, in addition to the objections elsewhere considered. It is probable, however, that college societies are not often mutual insurance companies; financially, at least, though they may perhaps be called such in other spheres.

Some of the principal moral advantages of the societies have now been considered. On these might possibly be based some claim to a good moral influence, if the society theory were not involved in such grave difficulties by its fundamental principle of secrecy.

This is a principle not at all calculated to promote either morality or religion. Though often perfectly innocent, it keeps such bad company

that it must always be challenged; above all,
when it is made systematic and perpetual. Secrecy may not always be wrong, but wrong-doing always tries to be secret. A secret system
does not develop the frankness and openness
which are among the best qualities of character.
Any one who compares the free openness of the
Anglo-Saxon race with the stealthy nature of
some other peoples will see why ex-President
Woolsey declares secrecy "averse to the English character." College secret societies, says
Dr. Howard Crosby, "are pretenses, and thus at
war with truth, candor and manliness. However harmless in their actual operations or un-
dertakings, however well composed in their
membership, however pure their meetings may
be, the fact of secrecy is insidiously weakening
the foundations of frank truthfulness in the
youthful mind,"[1] Lieber gives the political
objections already quoted, as being "in addition to their preventing the growth and development of manly character, and promoting vanity."[2] John Stuart Mill says, "The moral sentiment of mankind in all periods of tolerably en-
lightened morality, has condemned concealment
unless when required by some overpowering
motive."[3] Single texts of Scripture are to be
quoted with care as to the context, but the following seems to be pertinent: "Woe unto them
that seek deep to hide their counsel from the
Lord, and their works are in the dark, and they

[1] College Secret Societies, published by Ezra A. Cook,
Chicago; p. 31.
[2] Civil Liberty, p. 135.
[3] Dissertations and Discussions, Vol. IV, p. 46.

say, Who seeth us? and who knoweth us?"[1]
Our Lord also seems to state a general principle
in this passage,[2] "Men loved darkness rather
than light, because their deeds were evil. For
every one that doeth evil hateth the light, neither
cometh to the light, lest his deeds should be re-
proved. But he that doeth truth cometh to the
light, that his deeds may be made manifest, that
they are wrought in God." A special objection
to secrecy is that it gives opportunity for immoralities. The more upright members of a
secret association are often overborne by the
others, while the pledges to secrecy and the supposed demands of honor prevent them from
using means to purify the association, or taking
the public action which would remedy matters. Dr. Crosby says,[3] "I do not speak ignor-
antly, but from a personal experience. Thirty
years ago I was a member of a college secret society, and, while I had upright fellow members,
and we encouraged literary culture, I found the
association was chiefly a temptation to vice.
The promise of secrecy prevented all disclosure
to parents, and the seclusion was thus perfect.
We met in a back room of a hotel, liquor was
brought from the bar-room for the company,
and, as in all such styles of association, the conversation gravitated to the obscene and the sens-
ual. At times the scene became painfully dem-
onstrative. I do not charge all or any of our
college secret societies with such excesses at this
day. Thirty years may have wrought a change.

[1] Isaiah XXIX : 15.
[2] John III : 19-21.
[3] College Secret Societies, as above ; p. 32.

The very society to which I belonged, I have reason to believe, at this time is perfectly free from these stains. But still they all offer a remarkable opportunity for sins, in which publicity would not allow their members to indulge for a moment."

Many of these organizations are said to teach morality. Apart from religion, as already observed, this may have no small value; but it is then off its true ground. It has lost the moral dynamic, the underlying divine personality which makes it a power, and so fails of its due influence among men. Even if heeded, it often becomes mere expediency, and so cannot be compared with that unselfish morality which is based on religion. The relation of the societies to Christian morality, as such, may properly be considered under their relation to the church.

CHAPTER VII.

I love thy church, O God !
Her walls before thee stand,
Dear as the apple of thine eye,
And graven on thy hand.
—*President Dwight.*

The church is the institution divinely ordained
for establishing the kingdom of God in the hearts
of men. It is in relation to this kingdom that
morality has its true meaning and value; and
the most important question connected with the
societies is their relation to the spiritual church
of God, and to the visible church which is its
outward expression.

Although the church is the true teacher of
morality, yet the societies might supplement her
efforts by their labors in teaching morality, as
many other institutions do practically, if not
purposely; but as a matter of fact their secret
and exclusive character unfits them for any such
office, while they tend to substitute a lower and
partial morality, in which the human element
predominates, for that higher law which has divine authority; thus taking the place of the
church.

The trouble here is much more serious when
these organizations are viewed as religious,
which many of them in some degree are. This
is advanced as an argument in favor of some
orders; but it actually is an argument against
them, for it leads men to put them in place of

the church.   In connection with city evangelistic
work, a frequent experience of the author has
been to have his invitation to meeting met with
the reply, "I go to the lodge," or, " My husband
belongs to two societies," as if that were quite
sufficient.   Now these societies can be of little
real value as substitutes for the church.   Including so many unconverted men, and men with
every sort of belief, their general religious exercises must be of a very formal and elementary
character; and though more special meetings
are sometimes held, as prayer-meetings in the
chapter houses in colleges, this is probably
very exceptional.   All church members, it is
true, are not very devout; but probably few
evangelical churches compare with the societies
as to the heterogeneous religious character of
their membership.   The latter therefore do harm
to the church, by putting in its place institutions
which have little or no real religion.   Partly
for this reason, partly because of the exclusive
character of the societies, the use of the Scrip-
tures and of religious ceremonies which they
often make is impious.   What is said of God's
people they often apply to members of their
own fraternity, leaving out the rest of us in a
way which makes us doubtful whether to be in-
dignant or amused.   Speaking of a deceased
member, they will allude to the "Great Com-
mander" who has called him to "a celestial
convocation of the infinite chapter," as though
the Almighty were the head of their order, and
heaven one of its chapters.   The feelings of dis-
gust which such sentiments inspire in other
Christians are chargeable to the system, because
they spring from its exclusive spirit.   College

societies, however, are probably religious only to a limited degree, if at all.

The influence of secret societies upon independence of character has already been noticed. The importance of this quality in the constitution of the moral character can hardly be overestimated. It is the keystone of the arch. It means loyalty to God and right rather than subservience to the opinions and customs of men, when these conflict. As such, it is one statement of the great comprehensive principle of obedience to God, which is the foundation of all Christian character. A large college teaches men how to live in communities with due regard to the opinions and rights of others; but it must also teach that independence which is grand and manly because it is founded in principle and its trust is in God.

The spirit of a secret society is not the catholic spirit of Christianity. It belongs to the old partial and exclusive systems of heathenism, a great number of which were themselves secret societies, like the Egyptian religion, the mysteries of Eleusis, and many parts of the Roman religion. So Lieber speaks of "the important fact that mysterious and secret societies belong to paganism rather than to Christianity."[1] When the vail of the temple was rent in twain, it signified that thenceforward the way into the holiest was freely open to all men everywhere, and that every man was himself to be a king and a priest unto God. This is the principle which is the foundation of modern civil and religious liberty. It was the spring of the Refor-

[1] Civil Liberty, p. 135.

mation; it is the inspiration of republicanism. How essentially the secret society spirit is at war with these principles may be seen from its very nature, perhaps, but especially from the spirit of such religious sentiments as have been put forth by some of the fraternities. Compare their narrow and exclusive spirit and purpose with the free and universal invitations of the Gospel, with the spirit of the church of Christ, that great institution whose doors stand open day and night, and whose welcome is as wide as humanity.

The principal distinction between men in this world is that between the converted and the unconverted, those who are Christians and those who are not. It is imperative on all Christians to recognize this great truth and act accordingly. If the salt has lost its savor, it is worthless. The world respects a decided Christianity, and is won to conversion by it much sooner than by that which shows a compromising spirit. The world is at war with God, and in such a contest compromise is impossible. It can never be lifted up to Christianity by taking the latter down to its moral level, and the church of Christ will never be the power which it might be, in college or anywhere else, until it stands uncompromisingly, without bigotry, indeed, but firmly, on the truth. Phillips Brooks gives the principle, though he probably would not make this application of it: " Fashionable society is neither intellectual nor spiritual; * any man or woman must break its chains and refuse to be its slave, or it is impossible to come to the best culture either of mind or soul."[1] A man must "put

[1] The Candle of the Lord and other Sermons, p. 213.

aside the lower that the higher may come in to him." At a Christian convention in Chicago, Mr. Moody said, " Separate yourselves from the world and the things of the world. God wants his people separate. They will have ten thousand times more influence when separate from the world. It is separation, not compromise that we want. The cry ought to be raised all over this Western country, '*Separation*, SEPARATION!' But people will say, If you take that stand—lift yourselves so high—a great many of these men will leave the church. Never mind. If we should lose some church members we shall gain many that are better men. Hundreds will come in and take their places. There should be no compromise." Dr. T. L. Cuyler said, in a late issue of the New York *Independent*, [1] " Christ's followers never will save the world by secularizing itself or surrendering its strict principles of loyalty to whatever is right and pure and holy. Conformity to the world will never convert it. 'Come out and be ye separate,' saith the Lord, "and touch no unclean thing.' * * Conformity to the world is weakening the backbone of the Church, and thus far diminishing its power to lift the world up toward God. 'If thou wouldst pull a man out of a pit,' said quaint old Philip Henry, 'thou must have a good foothold, or else he will pull thee in.'"

Paul gives the same principle, in a different connection, " Be ye not unequally yoked together with unbelievers; for what fellowship hath righteousness with unrighteousness? and what communion hath light with darkness?

[1] New York Independent, June 1, 1882.

And what concord hath Christ with Belial? or what part hath he that believeth with an infidel? * * Wherefore come out from among them, and be ye separate, saith the Lord, and touch not the unclean thing; and I will receive you, and will be a Father unto you, and ye shall be my sons and daughters, saith the Lord Almighty." [1] And our Lord says of his servants, "They are not of the world, even as I am not of the world." [2]

This truth has particular application on doubtful questions. It is the little foxes that destroy the vines, and the loss of character often begins in giving the inclination the benefit of the doubt. Mr. Moody's rule is the precise opposite, "Give your conscience the benefit of the doubt; even if you are mistaken, the Lord will bless you just the same." With the modification that the doubt must be a reasonable and well-established one, and not a mere whim or eccentricity, I believe this to be the true rule, whose adoption would save many a Christian from serious or fatal embarrassment, and make him a power for good.

What is meant by this teaching, however, must not be confounded with an ascetic or monastic view of life. It is to be noticed that nearly all those quoted above are men of a vigorous, aggressive type of piety, men of hearty whole-souled life, men, not of this world, who yet take a strong hold of things in it. It has been ordained that Christians are to be mingled with those who are not Christians in many of

[1] II Corinthians, VI: 14–18.
[2] John XVII: 16.

the relations and concerns of life. Such association develops Christian character, by trial of
it, and is also the means whereby the leaven of
Christianity is to work in society. The only
question is where such association involves compromise. Whether these principles exclude
Christians from secret societies or not, every
man must decide for himself, in his right of private judgment. My own opinion is that in most
cases they do. The objection here to a secret
society is that it involves a man as organizations
for a definite object, like societies for political
reform, for instance, do not. It somehow lays
claim to the whole personality, and creates too
close intimacies between persons of opposite
moral or religious character. In college societies this does some good, but more harm ;
though some men gain, others lose, and often
much more than enough to balance the first.
This is one great false principle in the society
theory ; the leading religious and moral men in
associations doubtful or more than doubtful,
closely bound up with men whose moral character is simply poison. Incalculable mischief
is often worked thus in college; the religious
leaders are so embarrassed that they do not lead,
and so no progress is made against the common
enemy, or there is a retreat. A college President says, "In some few instances, which have
come to our knowledge, a restraining moral influence has been exerted over young men who
were inclined to dissipation by their more serious
or religious associates in these societies, but we
fear that the effect is oftener to lower the tone of
religious character in the pious young men be-

longing to them."[1] Another President, " The literary and religious effect bad ; the moral effect equivocal—on good boys rather injurious—on bad boys rather beneficial. Membership lowers the tone of piety generally." A third, " The alienation of feeling and want of cordiality thus created are not favorable to a right moral and religious state."

There is a certain something about the society allegiance which seems to conflict with loyalty to the church ; and the Catholic church shows a true instinct on this point, as she does on many others, by forbidding her members to join any secret order without the church. Why this conflict should exist is not always clear ; certainly there is nothing of the kind about membership of a literary society, for instance. One reason for this may be found in the peculiar claim of the society to the whole personality of its members. The wearing of a badge signifies much more that membership of any other organization does. The society makes the same comprehensive claim which the church or the state or the family does ; a claim which has no such foundation in nature, and therefore operates to supplant the others.

Another reason for this may be found in the usual oaths, invoking the Deity to sanction obligations which are extra-judicial, and which unite Christians with unconverted men in a bond which is at least of doubtful character. Special objections also grow out of this, because the candidate may often be sworn to things which he does not approve of; or to vows of fraternal feeling which he cannot or will not try to keep.

[1] Hitchcock's Reminiscences of Amherst College, p. 323.

The societies often interfere with the practical workings of the church. They divide the members, in precisely the same way, and for the same reasons, as they divide the citizens of a state. A case once came to the writer's knowledge, of a man's refusing to join a certain church because he believed it to be run by a secret society. Church conferences are also sometimes believed to be controlled in the same way, and ministers are supposed to get or lose their positions because of society affiliations or antagonisms. How harmful all this is, not to the uniformity, which is not required, but to the real unity of the church, which is, needs no explanation. Here again, though political dissensions often work like serious results, yet with the societies there is danger of specially objectionable features of permanent jealousy and suspicion.

Reasons for this will perhaps appear more clearly if the formation of a secret society be imagined. Suppose the members of a church living in harmony and mutual affection, and then imagine the formation of a secret society among them. Is it not clear that such a change would be hostile to the spirit which had hitherto united them? Much forbearance would doubtless be exercised; but it is not altogether probable that feelings of bitterness and jealousy would arise? Of course few churches have reached a very perfect state of harmony; but in order to be approaching it they must keep obstacles out of the way, as far as possible. Some approach to it is almost necessary for any vigorous Christian life and work.

With college class societies, the divisive influence is especially felt. It operates very strongly to prevent that union among the Christian men in the different classes which is necessary for the best progress in Christian life and work. The reasons of this separation and its actual workings are the same in this sphere as they are in social and other relations already considered.

The course of the discussion thus far has shown that the secrecy and exclusiveness of the societies are serious objections to them, on social grounds, while the friendly and social relations of college life do not require them; that they destroy the college literary societies, taking only a small part of their place, and do not, on the whole, exert a wholesome intellectual influence; that their political influence is pernicious; that they are essentially aristocracies; and that they are generally hurtful both to morality and to the church.

CHAPTER VIII.

In multitude of counselors there is safety.—Solomon.

There is a considerable body of opinion which supports the positions taken in this discussion. Quotations may first be given from statesmen, or leading public men :

Washington is held up as belonging to a society, but with no great justice. Gov. Ritner quotes from Rev. Ezra Styles, D.D. :[1]

When Jonathan Trumbull was aid de camp to General Washington, he "asked him if he would advise him to become a Mason. General Washington replied that Masonry was a benevolent institution, which might be employed for the best or worst of purposes ; but that for the most part it was merely child's play, and that he could not give him any advice on the subject."

In a letter to Rev. Mr. Snyder, Washington corrects "an error you have run into, of my presiding over the English lodges in this country. The fact is, I preside over none, nor have I been in one more than once or twice within the last thirty years." [2]

Before his death he warned the country to beware of all secret societies.

John Hancock :

"I am opposed to all secret associations."

Samuel Adams :

"I am decidedly opposed to all secret societies whatever."

---

[1] Philadelphian, July 23, 1830.
[2] Letter dated Sept. 25, 1798, in Finney's Freemasonry, p. 222.

John Quincy Adams:

"I am prepared to complete the demonstration before God and man, that the Masonic oaths, obligations and penalties, cannot, by any possibility, be reconciled to the laws of morality, of Christianity, or of the land."[1]   April 10, 1833: "I do conscientiously and sincerely believe that the order of Freemasonry, if not the greatest, is one of the greatest moral and political evils under which this Union is now laboring."

Edward Everett:

"All secret societies are dangerous, in proportion to the extent of their organization and the number of their members. All secret associations, particularly all such as resort to the aid of secret oaths, are peculiarly at war with the genius of a republican government."

Judge Marshall, Chief Justice of the United States:

"The institution of Masonry ought to be abandoned, as one capable of producing much evil, and incapable of producing any good, which might not be effected by safe and open means."[2]

Horace Mann:

"It seems to me that all the higher and nobler instincts of mankind are adverse to such associations."

William H. Seward:

"I belong to one voluntary association of men, which has to do with spiritual affairs.   It is the Christian Church.   *
I belong to one temporal society of men and that is the political party.   *   *

These two associations, the one spiritual and the other temporal, are the only voluntary associations to which I now belong, or ever have belonged since I became a man ; and unless I am bereft of reason, they are the only associations of men to which I shall ever suffer myself to belong.

[1] Quoted from letter to Edward Livingston.
[2] Quoted from letter to Edward Everett.

Secret societies, sir ?   Before I would place my hand between the hands of other men, in a secret lodge, order,
class or council, and bending on my knee before them,
enter into combination with them for any object, personal
or political, good or bad, I would pray to God that that
hand and that knee might be paralyzed, and that I might
become an object of pity and even the mockery of my fellow
men.   •

Swear, sir !   I, a man, an American citizen, a Christian,
swear to submit myself to the guidance and direction of
other men, surrendering my own judgment to their judg-
ments, and my own conscience to their keeping ! No no, sir.
I know quite well the fallibility of my own judgment, and
my liability to fall into error and temptation.   But my life
has been spent in breaking the bonds of the slavery of men.
I, therefore, know too well the danger of confiding power to
irresponsible hands, to make myself a willing slave."

Daniel Webster, of Freemasonry :

" I have no hesitation in saying that however unobjec-
tionable may have been the original objects of the institution, or however pure may be the motives and purposes of
the individual members, and notwithstanding the many
great and good men who have from time to time belonged
to the order, yet, nevertheless, it is an institution which in
my judgment is essentially wrong in the principle of its
formation ; that from its very nature it is liable to great
abuses ; that among the obligations which are found to be
imposed on its members, there are such as are entirely incompatible with the duty of good citizens.   *   *   Under
the influence of this conviction it is my opinion that the
future administration of all such oaths, and the formation
of all such obligations, should be prohibited by law." [1]

Some more general testimonies are valuable.
One hundred seceding Masons, at LeRoy, New
York, during the Morgan excitement, said :

" We are opposed to Freemasonry because we believe :
*   *

It affords opportunities for the corrupt and designing to

[1] Letter dated Boston, Nov. 20, 1835.

form plans against the government, and the lives and characters of individuals.

It assumes titles and dignities incompatible with a republican government, and enjoins an obedience to them derogatory to republican principle.

It destroys all principles of equality by bestowing its favors on its own members, to the exclusion of all others, equally meritorious and deserving.

It creates odious aristocracies, by its obligations to support the interests of its members, in preference to others of equal qualifications."

A report to the United States anti-Masonic convention, in 1830, signed by Henry Dana Ward, of New York, Thaddeus Stevens, of Pennsylvania, Samuel C. Loveland, of Vermont, Joshua Longley, of Massachusetts, and G. P. McCulloch, of New Jersey, said:

" Russia, Spain, Portugal, Naples and Rome made Freemasonry a capital offense. There is no crime in the mummery to die for under the gallows ; the offense lies in the political use made of Freemasonry, dangerous to all governments. The sovereigns of France, England, Prussia, Netherlands, Sweden and Brazil, take the fraternity under the royal guardianship. This is not because their majesties love the farce of the lodge-room, but they fear its political tendency."

"The only countries in which Freemasonry flourishes, neither forbidden nor restrained, are the republics of North America. Here the growth is without a parallel (except in France, during the last years of Louis XVI.), a growth honorable to the freedom, but dangerous to the stability of our public institutions."

Some allowance is to be made on most of the above testimonies, and on some following ones because given during the Morgan excitement. In 1826 William Morgan,[1] of Batavia, New York, suddenly disappeared. Shortly afterward there

----

[1] Finney's Freemasonry, Ch. II.

was published a book, claiming to be an exposure by Morgan of the first three degrees of Masonry, which it undoubtedly was. It was pretty clearly proved that Morgan had been abducted by Masons, carried across the State, by an extended conspiracy, and confined in Fort Niagara. Here he disappeared, but in 1848 Henry L. Valance made a dying confession which has been quite generally believed, that he was one of three Masons, who took Morgan in a boat by night upon the river, tied him to several weights, and then pushed him with them over the side of the boat into the river. That he had been murdered by Masons was believed soon after his disappearance. This led to a tremendous national excitement. An anti-Masonic party was formed, which still exists, though very feebly, and of the fifty thousand Masons in the United States, forty-five thousand seceded from the order. The order is now, however, probably very large, as are some other secret associations.

There is also important testimony on religious grounds.

The one hundred seceders of LeRoy also adopted the following resolution against Masonry:

"It substitutes the self-righteousness and ceremonies of Masonry for real religion and the ordinances of the Gospel."

Rev. Chas. G. Finney, the great revival preacher, and president of Oberlin, who had been a Mason, says that after his conversion:

"I soon found that I was completely converted *from* Freemasonry *to* Christ, and that I could have no fellowship with any of the proceedings of the lodge. Its oaths ap-

peared to me to be monstrously profane and barbarous."[1]
" Its morality is unchristian.   *   Its oath-bound secrecy is
unchristian.   *   *   It is a virtual conspiracy against both
Church and State."

D. L. Moody :

" I do not see how any Christian, most of all a Christian
minister, can go into these secret lodges with unbelievers.
They say they can have more influence for good, but I say
they can have more influence for good by staying out of
them, and then reproving their evil deeds.   Abraham had
more influence for good in Sodom than Lot had.   If twenty-five Christians go into a secret lodge with fifty who are
not Christians, the fifty can vote anything they please, and
the twenty-five will be partakers of their sins.   *They are
unequally yoked with unbelievers.*   *   *   If they would
rather leave their churches than their lodges the sooner
they get out of the churches the better.   I would rather
have ten members who were separated from the world than
a thousand such members.   Come out from the lodge.
Better one with God than a thousand without Him.   We
must walk with God, and if only one or two go with us it is
all right.   Do not let down the standard to suit men who
love their secret lodges or have some darling sin they will
not give up."[2]

Twelve denominations "are committed by vote
of their legislative assemblies or by constitution
to a separation from secret lodge worship."
Among these are the Disciples (in part), who
number nearly six hundred thousand, the United
Presbyterians, eighty thousand, the Lutheran
Synodical Conference, five hundred and fifty
thousand, the Friends, about sixty thousand, the
German Baptists, or Dunker, sixty thousand, and
the United Brethren, one hundred and fifty thousand.   The total membership of these denominations is one million seven hundred thousand.

[1] Finney's Fremasonry, pp. 5, 262, 263.
[2] Farwell Hall, Chicago, Dec. 14, 1876.

"Individual churches in some of these should be excepted, in part of them even a considerable portion." Besides these, the Congregational "State associations of Illinois and Iowa, have adopted resolutions against the lodge," and many local churches also oppose the lodge. One article of the United Presbyterian Testimony, or creed, is:

"We declare that all associations, whether formed for political or benevolent purposes, which impose upon their members an oath of secrecy, or an obligation to obey a code of unknown laws, are inconsistent with the genius and spirit of Christianity, and church members ought not to have fellowship with such associations." [1]

The Discipline of the United Brethren still reads, I believe, as adopted in 1849:

"Freemasonry, in every sense of the word, shall be totally prohibited, and there shall be no connection with secret combinations (a secret combination is one whose initiatory ceremony or bond of union is a secret); and any member found connected with such society shall be affectionately admonished by the preacher in charge, twice or thrice, and if such member does not desist in a reasonable time, he shall be notified to appear before the tribunal to which he is amenable; and if he still refuses to desist, he shall be expelled from the church."

The United Brethren joined this with temperance and anti-slavery as making three great movements of moral reform; but it is now in many cases a dead letter, and will probably be taken out of the discipline. The majority will still hold to their convictions, but will adopt the principle of the great evangelical churches that these questions of moral reform are chiefly for the individual conscience.

[1] United Presbyterianism, p. 141.

As an expression of undergraduate opinion, an editorial in the Yale *Courant* of March 23, 1878, is so able and fair as to make it worth quoting entire:

" The recent stealing of chains from the Bones' fence, the breaking of their padlocks, and the confiscation of their supper, were expressions of a feeling not only sour but weak and mean. The taking of chains from the Keys' fence, also, was the outcrop of a temper just as small and pitiable. Strange that the popular attitude toward the Senior societies is either bitterness or idolatry ; bitterness if you know you cannot go, idolatry if you dream you can ; bitterness if you did not go, idolatry if you did. Thanks to the signs about college that a true neutral spirit is growing, a neutral spirit which is not neutrality, but a fair and gentlemanly independence, a neutral spirit which is not ashamed of itself, and which does not have to go begging for respect. Opposition to Bones and Keys is by no means a sin, we have even thought it a virtue, but when such opposition cankers into violence and acted malice, it becomes as much a crime as under-class subservience and fawning. We have no hopes of ever seeing the downfall of the Senior societies, those fascinating vampires of darkness, whose shadows fall ominously down the stairway of the academic years, and awe the climbers by the majesty of—dumbness ! But we sincerely hope and pray that Yale may never see the time when no manly neutrals shall have minds of their own, and when no independent paper dares let a neutral say his uttermost say. Even were Bones and Keys such a blessing as they are claimed to be—in disguise, yet it would be a sorry day for the college when there should no longer exist in it lusty, honest neutrals, but only soreheads : it would be worse, indeed, than that a nation should have but one political party. Bones and Keys are a curse to the college ; they increase the expenses of a course already perniciously tending to extravagance, and influence, where they do not handle, by creating a college atmosphere of more royal and stylish living ; they furnish the chief incentive to that trickery which seams under-class life through and through, dividing it into castes and engendering in it those bitter and undying alienations which to this very day disfigure '78 as they did '76. They cause occasional incapacity on the crew and the nine—we will not say how lately they have done this. They often produce unjust promotion to the Glee Club, and they sometimes elect athletic officers without regard to brains or business. In all candor we say it, we do not think they put many rewards upon, nor many safeguards around, temperance and morality in college, nor do we think their example as salutary for sound morals as institutions of such pretensions might be, for it is not so many years, nay, not so many Thursday nights ago, that a certain well-known Senior group came from the hall to the campus—*drunk !* Yet it is not, in the main, against the thirty *men* that we inveigh ; the present thirty are for the most part splendid men, including the very best in the class ; it is against the *system* that we state these unexaggerated but disagreeable facts of influence and tendency. The men are not, in the main, vicious men, only so far as they are supporting a vicious system. So long as a few men, just few enough to be unjustly representative, are segregated from a class and by tradition gifted with certain social honors supposed to be the signs of distinguished though mysterious merit, just so long will there rise among the students a natural, though dangerous, competition for distinction, whose intensity will ever vary directly as the narrowness of the probabilities for success. Yet Bones and Keys are not an unmixed evil ; to meet a select coterie once a week, and over a cheerful spread to discuss college gossip, there to chat with several Professors who have just entered, or at the great convocations of autumn and commencement to meet many of the most scholarly, successful, or wealthy gentlemen of the land, reaching back to the classes of antiquity, this is certainly not a sin, *per se.* These are the *partial* influences of certain meetings on thirty men, but the influences of a system on a college are something disastrously different."

The following testimony includes the words of many eminent graduates and educators.

Francis Lieber :

" It would lead us too far from our topic were we to discuss the important fact that mysterious and secret societies belong to paganism rather than to Christianity, and we conclude these remarks by observing that those societies which may be called doubly secret, that is to say, societies which not only foster certain secrets and have secret transactions, but the members of which are bound to deny either the existence of the society or their membership, are schools of untruth ; and that parents as well as teachers, in the United States, would do no more than perform a solemn duty, if they should use every means in their power to exhibit to those whose welfare is entrusted to them, the despicable character of the thousand juvenile secret societies which flourish in our land, and which are the preparatory schools for secret political societies." [1]

George William Curtis, one of our very best and ablest public writers, says in *Harper's Monthly* for January, 1874 :

"The spring of this triumphant political Anti-Masonic movement was hostility to a secret society. Many of the most distinguished political names of Western New York, including Millard Fillmore, Wm. H. Seward, Thurlow Weed, Francis Granger, James Wadsworth, George W. Patterson, were associated with it. And as the larger portion of the Whig party was merged in the Republican, the dominant party of to-day has a certain lineal descent from the feelings aroused by the abduction of Morgan from the jail at Canandaigua. And as his disappearance and the odium consequent upon it stigmatized Masonry, so that it lay for a long time moribund, and, although revived in later years, cannot hope to regain its old importance, so the death of young Leggett is likely to wound fatally the system of college secret societies.

Every collegian knows that there is no secrecy whatever in what is called a secret society. * * Literary brotherhood, philosophic fraternity, intellectual emulation, these are the noble names by which the youth deceive themselves and allure Freshmen ; but the real business of the society is to keep the secret, and to get all the members possible from the entering class.

* * Earnest curiosity changes into *esprit du corps*, and the mischief is that the secrecy and the society feeling are likely to take precedence of the really desirable motives in college. There is a hundred-fold greater zeal to obtain members than there is generous rivalry among the societies

[1] Civil Liberty, p. 135.

to carry of the true college honors. And if the purpose be admirable, why, as Professor Wilder asks, the secrecy? What more can the secret society do for the intellectual or social training of the student than the open society? Has any secret society in an American college done, or can it do, more for the intelligent young man than the Union Debating Society at the English Cambridge University, or the similar club at Oxford? There Macaulay, Gladstone, the Austins, Charles Buller, Tooke, Ellis, and the long illustrious list of noted and able Englishmen were trained, and in the only way that manly minds can be trained, by open, free, generous rivalry and collision. The member of a secret society in college is really confined, socially and intellectually, to its membership, for it is found that the secret gradually supplant the open societies. But that membership depends upon luck, not upon merit, while it has the capital disadvantage of erecting false standards of measurement so that the *Mu Nu* man cannot be just to the hero of the *Zeta Eta*. The secrecy is a spice that overbears the food. The mystic paraphernalia is a relic of the baby-house, which a generous youth disdains.

There is, indeed, an agreeable sentiment in the veiled friendship of the secret society which every social nature understands. But as students are now becoming more truly "men" as they enter college, because of the higher standard of requirement, it is probable that the glory of the secret society is already waning, and that the allegiance of the older universities to the open arenas of frank and manly intellectual contests, involving no expense, no dissipation, and no perilous temptation, is returning. At least there will now be an urgent question among many of the best men in college whether it ought not to return."

Hon. William M. Evarts, Ex-Secretary of State, who graduated at Yale in 1837, spoke at the alumni dinner of 1873. The *Hartford Courant* said next day :

"He did good work to-day in speaking against the evil effects of secret societies—a subject which had been previously well handled by Mr. Van Sanford. * * There were hundreds of old graduates who agreed with the speaker when he advocated the revival of the old societies

7

and the suppression of the foolish secret clubs which have supplanted them."

The *Courant* also said editorially :

" The speakers at the Yale alumni meeting yesterday did well in entering their protest against the influence of the class secret societies in killing the two great rival debating societies, which were open to the members of all classes. * * Mr. Evarts, who has few equals and no superiors as a ready thinker and talker, attributes no small degree of his success to the training of these societies. * * Of late the secret societies, confined to classes, and seldom mustering more than twenty at any evening session, have monopolized the time and attention of the students and have destroyed the honored old societies. To the graduate of a few years, there is nothing more absurd than the importance which the undergraduate attaches to his society badge and secrets. * * Meantime, the secret society fosters snobbery and tends to create division among the best friends. * * It would be a good thing if young men had the manliness to appreciate the bad effects of these societies and to voluntarily repudiate them and revive the more honorable and more manly rivalry of the great, open, college debating societies."

The *Springfield Republican*, Oct. 23, 1873 :

In earlier times, "Secret associations were an economical device. * * To-day and here they have no such excuse for their existence. There is not a moral, political or social purpose which secrecy can aid more than openness. * * It is a foible that belongs to the juvenile mind and the juvenile state of civilization. It is the meat of petty rather than large minds, and we fear we must say of the feminine rather than of the masculine cast of thought. Secret societies, therefore, thrive among vealy youth in colleges, and among a class of ordinary people who are just below politics."

President Robinson, of Brown, in his report to the corporation for 1876, mentions several objections to the societies, and closes by saying :

" That they are, as now existing with us, a direct hindrance to the best kind of work, I have no doubt."

President Hitchcock, of Amherst, gives letters from nine college Presidents on this point. [1] The first says :

"Could these associations be altogether removed from the institutions of learning in our country, I should think it a result in which friends of learning, 'and especially the officers of colleges, would have great occasion to rejoice."

A second President :

"As soon as the Faculty ascertained that such societies were in existence, they ordered the students to break off their connection with them, stating explicitly that they could not and would not be permitted."

A third President :

"We are unanimously and decidedly of opinion that it would be desirable to have all these secret societies rooted out of our colleges."

A fourth President :

"The literary and religious effect bad ; the moral effect equivocal. * * I have made one, nay more than one ineffectual attempt to rid this college of their influence. So far as I have seen, all direct opposition has only aggravated the evil ; and latterly my efforts have been directed to the modification and direction, rather than to the extermination of these societies, which I have always regarded as an evil —latterly as an evil inseparable from an assemblage of young men—perhaps of men of any age."

A fifth President :

"On the whole, my opinion is that they have been evil, and sometimes very much so. * * I suppose it would be desirable that secret societies should be rooted out of our colleges and from every other place. If all these paltry and rival associations could be at once and forever broken up there can be no doubt it would be a great blessing."

[1] Reminiscences of Amherst College, pp. 320–326.

A sixth President:

" There is reason to believe that some, at least, of those societies, have on the whole an injurious influence. * * There are altogether too many of them."

A seventh President:

" I am of opinion that the tendency of such societies is bad of necessity, that is, so long as they have the power, by means of secrecy, of doing mischief."

An eighth President:

" The only secret society * * known to exist here is supposed to be harmless, and its meetings are permitted to be held."

A ninth President:

" Their influence not suspected at first, but found to be bad. * * Nothing but evil results, or is likely to result from them upon members themselves as students, or as Christians, and no good to those who are not members. They are a mere plague to any college."

President Hitchcock, however, adds:

" We did not find it necessary to take any active measures against these societies, and they have been suffered ever since to exist. And I am confident that the evils feared from them have much diminished."

Dr. Howard Crosby, Chancellor of the University of New York, under the title of " My Objections to Secret Societies in Colleges," writes in the *Congregationalist* of 1869:

" The heart of man loves secrecy, because it is an element of power. * * Solid, studious men get this power in a legitimate way. * * Hidden treasures lie within their minds, and the world pays respect to the power that is implied. * * Where men cannot gain this position of influence in the legitimate way, either from want of capacity, or indolence, or the necessities of youth, there is a very natural endeavor to gain it by trick and assumption.

* * We have no hesitation in writing secret societies among the quackeries of this earth, a part of the great system by which the mud-begotten try to pass themselves off as Jove-born. Leave out those secret associations, whose concealment is for safety, as in political crises, and a secret society is a deception, more or less innocent according to the character of its contents.

My first objection to the secret societies of our colleges is founded on the above considerations. They are pretenses, and thus at war with truth, candor and manliness. ' *Omne ignotum pro magnifico*' is the principle from which they draw their life. * * Everything that conflicts with" truthful openness "is a sham and will leave its mark upon the character. A sham is not only in itself a mean thing, but it blocks the way to truth. * *

My second objection to secret societies in our colleges is in the opportunity given by the secrecy to immoralities. * * They all offer a remarkable opportunity for sins, in which publicity would not allow their members to indulge for a moment. * *

A third objection " is that " the confidence between parent and child is broken, and hence destroyed, by these secret societies. * * A free and entire communion between the young and their parents is both the safeguard of the young and the comfort of the parents. This the secret societies of our colleges overthrow. * * The secrecy of the college society renders it peculiarly adapted to be a rival to the family. * *

These are my three main objections to secret societies. * * But there are other local objections that belong to the college.

* * My fourth objection is, that college secret societies interfere with a faithful course of study. * * I always found the best students were those who either kept out of the secret societies, or who entered very slightly into their operations. * *

A fifth objection is found in the natural use of these societies for disturbance of public order. * * Out of the darkness dark deeds grow. * *

The sixth objection I have to offer is their evil influence upon the regular literary societies of the college, which are instituted as adjuncts of the curriculum. * * I believe that I am right in asserting that in most of our colleges the literary societies * * have been utterly ruined, except as alumni centers, by the secret societies.

My last objection is their expensiveness. * *

I know that many excellent men, long after they leave
college, support these societies. * *   But for all that, I
cannot but believe that the principle on which they rest is
pernicious, and nothing is gained by them which might not
be gained far better by open dealing.   The principle is not
only pernicious, but childish."[1]

Reports from forty-eight schools and colleges
in twenty states, as to college secret societies,
were sent to Ezra A. Cook & Co., Chicago, at
their request, about the year 1873.   Of these
only three expressed views favoring the societies, and the letters showed "a general and deeply
seated conviction that their nature and tendency
is wholly evil."

Among the institutions which do not allow
secret societies are many Western colleges, including Olivet, Beloit, Ripon and Oberlin.
They are forbidden at West Point.   In 1857 the
Princeton societies were suppressed by the
Faculty.   The same step was also taken at the
same time by the authorities at Harvard; a letter has been published elsewhere which shows
the position of a part of the Harvard Faculty
on this point.

The Yale Faculty have also committed themselves on this question.   Some years ago a part
of the incoming Sophomore class, which included in its number many of the best men in
the class, asked the Faculty to allow them to
form a society for the coming year.   The following are the conditions on which permission was
granted; they are given from memory, but may
be relied on as substantially correct:

[1] College Secret Societies, published by Ezra A. Cook,
Chicago; pp. 30-35.

1. The society shall not take the name of any previously existing society.

2. The society shall hold its meetings in some (I think public) room on the college campus.

3. The members of the Society shall wear no common badge.

4. The society shall give out no elections to members of succeeding classes.

These conditions would require a revolution in the society system, as it is at present. If a society composed largely of men of high standing in the Sophomore class were required to observe such conditions, it is a plain inference to the judgment of the Faculty upon the secret society system.

President Dwight's great name I find quoted against secret societies.

President Porter's position may be inferred from the following passage :

" The love of secrecy and reserve is too strong in human nature, and especially in boyish nature, to be easily thwarted. We doubt the expediency, because we disbelieve in the possibility of destroying or preventing secret societies. That such societies may be, and sometimes are, attended with very great evils, is confessed by the great majority of college graduates." [1]

Notice that the reason here suggested for allowing secret societies is that they cannot be prevented; not that they ought to be encouraged, or that they are a good thing.

Ex-President Woolsey, who is as earnest in religion as he is great in political and social science, and whom our instructors are glad to honor as their instructor, says :

" I don't believe in secret societies, either in college or out of it."

[1] American Colleges, p. 195.

CONCLUSION.

Some further considerations may properly be noticed here, which relate especially to the secret system in colleges.

This question is particularly important in relation to personal character. It is sometimes said that if the societies are evil, there are greater evils; which may be true, but an error in the higher relations of life is often the parent of errors which run all the way down to grossness, as there is an intimate though not always necessary connection between skepticism and immorality. The indifference or slothfulness of to-day may mean the vice of to-morrow; or the loss of opportunities which might have saved others from ruin. This truth has special force of those whose character is forming. " As the twig is bent, the tree is inclined." " Better that " the child, says Ruskin, "should be ignorant of a thousand truths, than have consecrated in its heart a single lie." [1] Dr. Crosby says, "The Sophomore wears his badge, an emblem of a sham, and feels a glow of pride in supporting an hypocrisy. This language is not too strong to those who are accustomed to trace the great evils of our world to their germs, and who would strangle the tiger when he is a manageable cub. These little(?)divergencies from truth in children and youth become the gigantic frauds of great world-life by the simple action of time upon divergent lines of progress. There can be no

---

[1] Time and Tide, p. 107.

more important instruction inculcated on our young men than the necessity of truthful openness as the very warp of all virtue." [1]

The great educational institutions are so related to the national life as to make it imperative on them to give this question thorough consideration and conscientious action. They are the schools of the nation; for their graduates, generally speaking, are the leaders in the politics, the church, the literature of the nation, in all the spheres which make up the national life. Their sons are to shape the character and mold the institutions of their generation. They must teach language, science and philosophy; but far more must they instill into their students undying love of true friendship, simple truth, clean-handed patriotism, and pure religion. Whatever pollutions enter the stream, its fountain must be kept clear.

The societies may be a step toward a system combining more of the social with the intellectual than did the old literary societies, and better adapted to the varying natures of students than were two great literary institutions; they may be, but in order to meet the true principles they must be so greatly changed as to make it very doubtful if they are. Two great literary societies dividing all college may or may not be the ideal system; yet it seems certain that the true society must be neither secret nor exclusive, neither a political party nor an aristocracy, but must be based on the simple, natural principle of organization for a definite end, under

[1] College Secret Societies, published by Ezra A. Cook, Chicago; pp. 31, 32.

which the social element will come naturally into place. So far as graduates are concerned, I need not dwell on the obvious duty which they have to consider whether they are supporting, for their own pleasure, institutions which on the whole are hurtful to the students.

If the objections to the societies are so serious, why do they find support among so many men of character and eminence? One reason lies in the natural conservatism of mankind. Men generally take things as they are, and make the best they can out of them, for themselves; which of course is not the true principle, but it rules with many, and is strong with nearly all. Hence, if a system is once well established, it can exist under a heavy load of abuses for a long time. If Southern men had had their way, there would have been a great slave-holding empire in the South to-day; although everybody knows that slavery is a bad system economically and every other way.

Many have never really considered the matter. They find the system existing and go on as their predecessors have done and their fellows are doing, with no thought of change; and many shrink almost unconsciously from thinking of the matter, knowing that such thought may lead to convictions which they do not care to entertain. Even if they do consider it, many will conclude that the evils mean simply the abuse of a good thing in bad hands, which is common enough, unfortunately, and so cannot be helped. One instance came to the writer's knowledge, not long since, of a student's saying of a particular system of this kind, that he did not think it a good one, but saw no way of helping matters, and so would take his election with the rest. Ex-Mayor Colden, who has been already mentioned as a man much respected, who had held high Masonic honors, takes up this point : " It may be asked how it happens that I should have been so long a Mason and not until this time expressed my disapprobation of the institution. * * I began to question its utility long ago. * * When I was hardly twenty-one years of age I was initiated in a lodge in New York, which was distinguished for the respectability of its members. * * My confidence that they would not have done anything wrong induced me to pass through the required forms with very little—too little—consideration. A like deference for the example of others led me from step to step with the same inconsiderateness." [1] As to the example of Washington and other great men who were members of secret societies, " I should have been awed by their opinions could I be sure that these patrons, of whom masonry so justly boasts, deliberately examined the merits of the institution ; but when I reflect how many years of my life were passed before I gave the subject due consideration, I cannot but suppose that they, like myself, for a long time may have been content to rest on the example of their predecessors, and that they have left their successors free to express their opinions."

Much of the support, again, is only virtual, not active. Men have belonged to a society in younger days ; whatever its faults, there are few

[1] College Pamphlets, Yale Library, Vol. 91, Anti-Masonic Address to People of New York, pp. 22, 23.

who do not retain some affection for their society, and they also think that honor requires
them to support it, or at least say nothing which
may bear against it.   It is to be said, further,
that this does not decide the question, though it
has an important bearing upon it.   Almost
every bad system has had good supporters,
sometimes a great many of them.   Witness the
record made by so many good men on the subject of slavery.

The nature of a college community presents
some special difficulties in the way of reform,
where a system is once established.   The students are these who feel the evils most.   No man
really understands what this system means unless it exists among his equals or his superiors.
But the students are in college a very short time,
comparatively.   They come at an early age, when
few of them have any definite opinions on a subject like this.   Consequently, they are ready to
take the current ideas of their institution ; and
those who do not take these, often arrive at their
own conclusions so late as to make their influence
of little value.   Yet in some instances much has
been done by the students; and it certainly is
very greatly to be desired that they should
themselves think fairly and act rightly on this
question.   Probably a large part of the evils in
the present system could be made to disappear
simply by the removal of the one bar of secrecy.

Before closing, I wish to warn the societies,
and particularly the more earnest men, of whom
they include so many, that in refusing to reply
to these arguments they are leaving many a
conscientious young man, where this system is
dominant, to struggle with doubts of a very

grave kind, and perhaps to sacrifice his conscience to their inducements. If the ideas here set forth are wrong, they should be set right; and for the sake of the many young men to whom this is an important, if not a vital, question, I demand that if these conclusions are false, some of the able thinkers in the societies state why they are false, and what the truth is; and perhaps also they may lead us all to take part in extending the system, if it can be shown beneficial to mankind. If they include men who are public teachers, I ask them to teach the public on this question. The excuse of the societies' being secret cannot be taken; for though a defense would abate something of their strictness, they could discuss many general principles.

My present conviction, however, is that this is an abominable system; could it be swept from every college campus and every community in the land, I believe there would be reason for great rejoicing. Would that some mighty blast could open all this secrecy and darkness to the free winds of thought and the sunshine of God's truth! But the question for those who oppose the system which has been discussed is not whether it can be entirely abolished, in the first instance, desirable as they may think such a result; but whether matters cannot be so changed that it shall lose some of its objectionable features, or at least cease to be the system which is dominant over everything. There seems to be no reason why such a change may not be brought about; but there are difficulties to be met, and it might take time. It would be one step in the general progress of the colleges toward more true and manly ideas of college life.

As the earth turns toward the sun in her course, and his kindly influences soften for all good seeds and growths the frost-bound soil, which no instrument of steel could make fertile, so may the minds of the young men of this generation turn toward the greater Sun of truth, and be made ready for larger and nobler and more generous thinking and living in the light of His coming day.

www.ingramcontent.com/pod-product-compliance
Lightning Source LLC
Chambersburg PA
CBHW032147010726
47493CB00008BA/2621